Jessica Carried Zach's Child.

But at this time, he must not know about the baby. Such a revelation was too soon for him. How could she lure him into commitment at a time like this? What would people think?

She watched him, sternly cautioning her body to behave. While she didn't remember being the "wild" woman he claimed, she did remember that she'd—participated.

It had been...wonderful.

She slid her eyes discreetly down his body. It could happen again. One more time...

Dear Reader,

Can you believe that for the next three months we'll be celebrating the publication of the 1000th Silhouette Desire? That's quite a milestone! The festivities begin this month with six books by some of your longtime favorites and exciting new names in romance.

We'll continue into next month, May, with the actual publication of Book #1000—by Diana Palmer—and then we'll keep the fun going into June. There's just so much going on that I can't put it all into one letter. You'll just have to keep reading!

This month we have an absolutely terrific lineup, beginning with *Saddle Up*, a MAN OF THE MONTH by Mary Lynn Baxter. There's also *The Groom, I Presume?*—the latest in Annette Broadrick's DAUGHTERS OF TEXAS miniseries. *Father of the Brat* launches the new FROM HERE TO PATERNITY miniseries by Elizabeth Bevarly, and *Forgotten Vows* by Modean Moon is the first of three books about what happens on THE WEDDING NIGHT. Lass Small brings us her very own delightful sense of humor in *A Stranger in Texas*. And our DEBUT AUTHOR this month is Anne Eames with *Two Weddings and a Bride*.

And next month, as promised, **Book #1000, a MAN OF THE MONTH,** *Man of Ice* **by Diana Palmer!**

Lucia Macro,
Senior Editor

Please address questions and book requests to:
Silhouette Reader Service
U.S.: 3010 Walden Ave., P.O. Box 1325, Buffalo, NY 14269
Canadian: P.O. Box 609, Fort Erie, Ont. L2A 5X3

Lass Small

A STRANGER IN TEXAS

SILHOUETTE *Desire*®

Published by Silhouette Books

America's Publisher of Contemporary Romance

To: Teri Letizia
My vital medical consultant

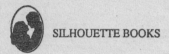 SILHOUETTE BOOKS

ISBN 0-373-05994-9

A STRANGER IN TEXAS

Copyright © 1996 by Lass Small

This edition published by arrangement with Harlequin Books S.A.

® and TM are trademarks of Harlequin Books S.A., used under license. Trademarks indicated with ® are registered in the United States Patent and Trademark Office, the Canadian Trade Marks Office and in other countries.

Printed in U.S.A.

LASS SMALL

finds living on this planet at this time a fascinating experience. People are amazing. She thinks that to be a teller of tales of people, places and things is absolutely marvelous.

Dear Reader,

It is a cherished honor to be included in Silhouette Desire's **Celebration 1000.** This is a good time to mention that I've been very fortunate in the skilled editors to whom I've been assigned. Thanks to them all and to Marcia Book Adirim now.

A Stranger in Texas is a different book. It is one of widely varying emotions that are funny and earnest. It is about living and about sharing lives with compassion. The story takes place in a fictional small town above the real city of Corpus Christi, TEXAS, and it concerns the adjustments made between those who are living there.

The book was interesting to write, and it will give a reader an insight into other aspects of life.

I am very grateful to my neighbor, Teri Letizia, to whom this book is dedicated. Teri is my medical consultant. She is a gem. There are Teri's clear, instant replies to my questions. Then she gives me more. She tells me of wider ramifications that I wouldn't have thought to inquire about or even to wonder about.

All of the books I've sent to Silhouette have pleased me. *A Stranger in Texas* is another. See if you agree.

With writer's love,

Lass

One

While Texas has been occupied by Europeans for the past five hundred years, it's been relatively recently that the northerners have been called Winter TEXANS. They had been known as Snow Birds, like the regular birds who fly south to get away from winter. The humans' labeling was changed to Winter TEXANS when the druggies gave a new meaning to the word "snowbird."

Winter TEXANS are welcomed wholeheartedly. They are lured to stay. And Sea View was one such place that lured them.

Sea View's big hotel was called The Horizon. The town was north of Corpus Christi on the TEXAS coast. Sea View wasn't on many of the maps.

The hotel had been built with wild expectations when the seacoast boom began long ago. Somehow that spot above Corpus had been lost to the general tourist bunch and bypassed for Padre Island by the college kids.

Even the main coastal highways had gone around Sea View. The town fathers hadn't had the clout nor the money to get the highway to bend their way. The road builders placidly said it was illegal to go through the environmentally protected sand dunes with another road. Keeping the sand from shifting was another nuisance.

Why were all those problems listed for Sea View and not for Padre Island? At Padre, there was a four-lane highway down the center of that sand bar. No one ever knew the reason Sea View couldn't just have a two-laner split from the main highway with a good direction sign.

Of course, there was already a road to the town of Sea View. It was a local two-laner that meandered along the path of least resistance. The highway people said that was sufficient.

With The Horizon Hotel and the elegant hospital, everybody in Sea View had predicted, "Just watch. As soon as we've had a flock of guests here, the word will spread. We'll be swamped with tourists. We'll get that highway split here."

The natives had been disgruntled, until they saw how the non-TEXANS had lighted on Padre like pushy buzzards. By then, most of the citizens were glad this hadn't happened to their own town.

Well, not everybody was glad. There were the sitters on the square who speculated what their land would have brought them and how they would then be living. There were guffaws over that—they'd just be sitting gossiping somewheres else. The whole, entire debate was just more wasted time.

However, through the years The Horizon Hotel had gradually gathered a following of very nice people who came especially in winter for the pleasure of just being on the coast and breathing the clean Gulf breeze that tumbled their hair. And they went out on boats or stood in the surf to fish or they played in or walked along the sand, collecting shells under the TEXAS winter sun.

Sea View native Jessica Channing was, by then, twenty-nine years old. In another year, she'd be an old maid. She was redheaded and green-eyed, and she didn't give one hootin' hot damn about getting married.

Her sister and brother were both married and had enough children to distract the parents from their youngest, unwed child.

Jessica had observed too many failed marriages. She didn't need that kind of problem. She lived as she wanted, spent as she wanted and ate when she wanted, what she wanted. Her brother told her she was getting staid and persimmonish.

She agreed.

Jessica was the accountant at the Horizon Hotel. Her life was neat and orderly. She knew everyone in town. That wasn't difficult. She knew all the secrets... and those secrets she knew, she never mentioned.

She was tall enough and well made. Her complexion was the ivory of real redheads, and her green eyes were gorgeous, deep, seeing into souls.

Jessica made people straighten up and quit gossiping. There was just something about her that shivered them a little. Maybe it wasn't them so much as it was their consciences. Jessica never gossiped, but they did. She made them feel as if she was better than they.

Being a paragon was something of a burden. Jessica did understand her position. She was not only good with balancing books and straightening out tangles in thinking, but she was also breathtakingly beautiful.

That's always a burden for a woman. Any smart woman knows being beautiful causes all sorts of problems with other women. Men, too, are a real nuisance, but women are leery of beautiful women. They avoid including them.

What woman wants that kind of competition?

While a man always wants the best woman possible, he rarely knows what to do with one. He is inclined to either worship her—and always be underfoot—or he ignores her to prove he's not her slave. But men are competitive. They do try. They are a real exasperation.

The town of Sea View not only had the remarkable hotel that functioned nicely, but they had that hospital. It was the only one in the whole area. It had been built on the same exuberant wave ride as the hotel. It was as popular as the hotel!

The staff was superior. They were lured by the sea, the beaches, the golf course, the small townness and the gossip. It was as if all those outsiders belonged. And the staff was always amazed over how distant were the homes of those who were brought there to be healed, or rearranged or fixed.

People did amazing things. They fell down stairs, crashed gliders, survived plane wrecks and whatever else people found to half kill themselves. It is always appalling when people are harmed on a highway, or worse on a byway.

This is a civilized and crammed country. But even now, there are those places that are very, very isolated.

And things do happen.

There were still tales of who and why various patients had been brought to Sea View. They came to the hotel called The Horizon. And some needed that unusual hospital soberly named Medical Center.

A good many of the people so introduced into the area, via the hospital, came back to vacation at The Horizon.

It was called so because, looking on beyond, that was about all you could see.

But like the rest of TEXAS, the view to the Gulf of Mexico was always unique, with the changing of the sky's colors and the winds. There were the cloud formations and the moving seawater. Far out were the big ships. Closer by were the fishing boats.

Wherever one looked, it was always different. It took a peculiar person to be bored at Sea View.

In the town, the seafood served was simply remarkable. And there was always the Mexican food. Even so, more discreet foods were available to any picky appetites.

To walk off the excellent foods, there was the golf course, and there was the beach. There were the shells to gather.

The shell necklaces were easy to string. A sea worm liked the muscle in the tiny shells. The hole it bored to get to the muscle was perfect for the shells to carry a string.

Everything contributes to everything else. Even us.

When Zachary Thomas's car was hit by a speeding pickup coming around a dune on the wrong side of the road, it happened in the middle of nowhere. The truck driver had not buckled his seat belt and was killed instantly. A good way for him to avoid the whole, ensuing mess.

But Hannah Thomas was killed as quickly. Even knowing she had to be dead, it seemed to her husband Zachary that he could feel her pulse.

Was it her pulse that hammered, or only his own?

His cellular phone had been smashed. Tears leaked from his eyes without his knowing; he wept in appalled frustration.

His twelve-year-old son Michael's heart still beat, but he was totally out of it. He was so limp and helpless.

There had been no habitation along the road. Zach quickly climbed a sand dune and looked—at more sand dunes.

He wasn't sure which way to go for help. He could not leave his family. He went back to them. He stood in the roadway and urged God to send help to his helpless ones.

It seemed to take much longer than it actually did.

Finally a car screeched its brakes as it came around the bend and found the crunched truck, the car...and the bodies.

It was Sea View's Paul Butler who swung open his car door and got out. His quick eyes recognized that the driver of the truck was gone from this land of the living. Then the newly arrived Paul looked at the stunned man standing by the other car. "You okay?"

"We need help. Can you get—"

"I got a CB. You oughta have one."

Zack explained, "My phone was smashed."

"Those things don't do good in wrecks."

In the time the man talked into the receiver, seemingly so aloof, he was checking the three people who could not speak.

When he finished with the CB, the stranger came to Zachary and talked to him, evaluating his condition. "It's best to wait. My name's Paul Butler," Paul told the man called Zachary Thomas. "We could do more harm if we was to try to get him—them to the hospital. Let's let somebody do it that knows how."

"Yes."

And since the stranger seemed on the verge of shock, Paul went on carefully, "You traveling?"

"We're still some distance from Corpus."

"They'll take hi—'em to the hospital in Sea View. It's not far. The hospital is a good one. And there's a good hotel there. The Horizon. It's called that because that's all you see." Paul spoke slowly. "But when you look out, the colors of the water and the clouds are a beautiful sight."

"Sea View? Is it on the map?"

"Not very many," Paul replied as he shook his head. "The map has to be pretty current and specific to get Sea View on it." He slid his eyes over to the woman who was so dead. The man held her hand.

"You been to TEXAS much?" Paul asked.

"This is our first time."

"It's a shame Ike got in your way thisaway."

Zach looked up at Paul and blinked. "You know him?"

"Yeah, I did. He always drove like a bat out of hell. I don't think they insure him anymore, but your insurance ought to be okay. You got some, don't you." It was a statement.

"Yes."

"You look the careful type. I'll go to court with you and explain how this happened."

Within Zach, some thread of curiosity made him ask, "You would testify for me?"

"Sure. I've known Ike all his life long. He's one hairy driver. Or he was one. No more. He's bought the farm."

"He bought a farm?"

"It's just an expression. His life insurance will pay the bills."

Zach had been looking at Paul, but then he looked down at his wife and at his son.

The distant siren came almost immediately. Neither man spoke. The sound came closer, louder. It was a surprise that it came around the bend slowly. It was a moxie driver who knew to be careful.

Quickly, the men checked out the bodies, and it was the boy whom they stabilized, lifted onto a stretcher and took into the ambulance. They looked at Paul, who nodded minimally, then he asked Zach, "You okay?"

"Yeah."

"You going with the boy?"

Startled, Zach asked, "What about Hannah?"

And his expression was such that one man said to the other, "We can fit her in." Then they carefully, needlessly stabilized her head and put her on another stretcher.

The highway police arrived by then and told Zach to go along with Paul. They'd see them at the hospital.

Paul stayed with Zach for the time left of that day. He was a rock. He led Zach through everything very discreetly, including a check on his condition. Zach didn't mention his headache. He thought it was stress. The medical people weren't fooled.

To Zach, Paul was a godsend. How could such a casual man, as Paul was, be so knowledgeable? He knew what a victim of circumstances in a strange place needed.

Paul asked, "Would you want to see the minister?"

"Not now."

When the doctor finally came out to Zach, he asked, "You been looked at? Are you all right?" And he frowned at Zach.

"Yeah."

The doctor said, "You may have guessed it already and right away that Hannah didn't make it. She did not suffer. It happened instantly."

It only confirmed what Zach had suspected. He was silent for a while. So was the doctor. And so was Paul, who was there.

Peripherally, even then, Zach was aware of Paul's empathy and presence.

Finally, Zach asked about his son. "How is my boy?"

The doctor replied, "It doesn't look good. His pupils are dilated and don't react to light. We've done the first EEG, which measures brain waves. Those next two tests will be at twelve-hour intervals. That's to test whether the brain is functioning. We'll have to wait for tomorrow.''

With the pupils fixed and dilated, those at the hospital already were sure, but the doctor knew that two such blows might be too much for this torn man. "Would you like to sleep here? You may. But I would advise you to go to the hotel where it will be more restful. Come with me to see Michael, now. Then decide where you want to sleep.''

Paul asked Zach, "Want me along?''

Zach turned to look at the stranger who was a substitute guardian angel. The man was silent and unintrusive. Zach said, "Please.''

They went to the emergency room and there lay Michael. A budding man. He lay there with myriad tubes and monitors connected to him. The lung machine pumped air. The stem of his brain kept his heart beating. Mike was still and peaceful.

And Zach knew. He asked the doctor, "There is no hope at all?''

He hadn't planned to tell the father until the next morning. There was no getting around it. "We need two more EEG's. The third will be tomorrow morning.''

"Yes.''

"We hope for a miracle. It may not come.''

"I...understand.'' Pain washed over Zach's alive body. It was reality. Then he asked, "May I see Hannah once more? Or have they taken her?''

"She's here. Would you like to be alone with her for a while?''

"Yes.''

The doctor led the way down the hall to the room where Hannah lay so quietly. His voice was level as he told the stunned husband, "While your wife's organs were oxygen-dead, most of Michael's vital organs can be used. We call it organ harvesting. This is something for you to consider. You can allow Michael to give the gift of life to other people. Think on this."

Then steadily the doctor told Zach, "We know what you've gone through. We understand your situation of decisions. It's a tough place for anyone to stand. If we can help you in any way, ask us. We are all here for you."

It was Paul who stood silently with his hand on Zach's shoulder. But Zach went alone to sit by his wife. Once he asked her, "Is Mike with you? Is he here?"

There was no reply in the silence.

Zach finally left the room and didn't even notice that Paul had waited and then followed Zach only to the door when he went to his son.

Michael looked as peaceful as Hannah. Zach resented their peace. How could they leave him there...alone? To have been a family, one of three for so long and now to be alone.

But they had been so badly hurt. How could he resent their escape? The air bags hadn't worked with the slant of the car crash. Hannah had hit her head on the window. A neat, lethal blow.

With the companionship they'd shared for all those years, she'd left him without a word. How would it be to again be alone?

At least the two would be together. Zach leaned and kissed his son's forehead.

Zach left the room, and Paul was still a shadow.

Paul said logically, "We need some milk to soothe us. Let's go to the hotel and get you signed in."

It was almost six o'clock, but there in the hotel lobby office was Jessica Channing. She came to the empty desk and said, "I'm substituting for Vera. What can I do to help you?"

Paul smiled, but Zach didn't even see Jessica. He was going into something similar to shock. His heart pumped and his breathing picked up. It was a form of delayed panic.

Jessica said to Paul, "Is this Zachary Thomas?"

"Yeah, he's had it."

"I understand. He needs to walk for a while. We'll get him a glass of milk."

Paul asked, "Could you walk with him? He needs somebody along. I've got to check in at home."

"Rick said you found them. I called Sue. The kids are wild, and you need to go home. I'll go with him."

Zach understood nothing. He was not only in some panic but in shock. Things had happened that he couldn't prevent. He couldn't stop them. He'd flubbed it. They were both . . . gone! How could they be?

Someone came silently with the glass of tepid milk. Paul took it and handed it to Zach, who didn't pay any attention because his mind was in a distraction of disorientation.

He drank the milk down and set the glass on the reception counter, and Jessica said, "Let's walk."

They went out of the hotel and across the entrance road to the sand. They turned north along the wet, solid beach just above the receding waves. They didn't speak at all. They walked.

The surging waves were soothing. There weren't too many people around. The breeze was fresh. It played in their hair and ruffled their clothing. The sun was low in the western sky. Around Zach the air was silent of voices and no decisions pushed at him. He was free.

Helping people in shock was one of the things the town of Sea View had learned. Of course, there were a few people who didn't volunteer at the hospital. To the rest, it was interesting and they helped. They were that kind of people.

The shocked man with the woman stranger at his side didn't walk far. Jessica knew better than to exhaust a person in his position. But he was then outside and free. It gave the feeling of control to the man. Lured into walking, in his shock, he now felt walking on the beach had been his idea. He was in control.

By then, they were back at the hotel. He was given a sedative to take if he chose. Paul's note said the doctor recommended it. Zach needed to rest. Tomorrow would be a tough day.

Zach read Paul's note and looked at Jessica. "Paul has been a rock for me this afternoon." His own voice sounded apart from him. "I don't know how to thank him for all that time. For that support."

"You can tell him tomorrow." Jessica told Zach that so easily. She knew what a hell of a day the next day would be. The boy had no chance at all. The harvesters would gather from the airport with their little ice buckets. They would be sober-faced, earnest and grateful.

They would harvest bone, heart, kidneys, eye lenses and skin. The harvesting was generally within the state. Michael's gifts would help people all over TEXAS.

Jessica told Zach, "Do take the pill. It will help your body relax. You need the rest."

And Zach said, "Take me to my room. I'm not sure I can make it on my own."

Jessica looked at that man. How many times had she heard something similar?

He was serious. He was wrung out.

Even later, she considered that she could have easily gotten someone else to take him to his room. He wouldn't turn a hair because his request had been so vulnerable. He was not a lecher.

She looked at the clock on the wall. Vera would be back in about ten minutes. Jessica told Don, "Watch the desk?"

Don eyed the man beside Jessica with gradually diminishing suspicion. "Sure. I'll call Vernon to take up his luggage." Don looked around but there was none.

Zach replied, "It's in the car and the car's probably been hauled to someplace else. I was in a wreck."

Only he. Only he was wrecked. The others had survived in a different way. They'd escaped from life. He was alone.

Or—had he died, too, and was he just around as a haunt? He hadn't wanted to die, and his mind had prevented it? He would come to his ghost's limit in time, and he'd just...leave? Why hadn't he gone with them? Why was only he there? Was he alive?

He looked at Jessica. She was probably his imagination. She was unreal, she was so beautiful. He'd drawn her from adolescent dreamings. Hannah had been the real woman, a good friend; this one was a dream.

Jessica collected a shaving kit and a shirt from the gift shop. She found socks and underwear. She brought them back to Zach. He heard himself say, "Put it on my bill."

And she replied, "We'll see."

His eyes slitted as he studied her in the half light of the fading day. Yeah. She was a dream. He was probably at the side of the road...in the wrecked car...still.

He asked the iridescent woman, "Are you real?"

And she realized he was in shock. He was working on only half a brain. She said soothingly, "We all are."

Not all.

She said, "Come." And she led the way to the elevator. She had the key and carried the other things she'd gathered for him.

He followed, observing her walk. She had a good walk. She barely moved but her skirts did. They swayed. He blinked and looked away from her. The evening lights were dimmed by the setting sun. The hazed atmosphere was ethereal... It was weird.

They were the only ones in the elevator. As in a dream, they were alone. Such isolation was a part of a dream. The redhead would disappear...when they got to his bed.

People weren't going to their rooms, they were going down the elevators to the dining rooms, but it seemed a dream to Zach.

The pair reached his floor. Jessica located his room on the discreet gold rectangle with black lettering and numbers. She compared the key and told him, "From the elevator, you turn left."

He replied, "Yeah." And he looked at her face. He was taller than she. He was a dominant male. How strange to feel that. He'd always thought of women as equals. The wreck had thrown him back into his basic male thinking. He was dominant.

At his room, it was Jessica who unlocked his door. She opened it inward, effortlessly, and he seemed to drift beside her into the room.

She looked around. It was very neat and orderly. She checked the bath and it, too, was pristine.

The accommodations were always that way.

Jess went to the bureau and opened the drawer to put in his newly purchased underwear. She removed myriad straight pins from the new shirt. She got them all. She would. Then she hung the shirt in the closet.

She put his shaving kit in the bathroom.

Then she came back into the bedroom with a glass of water, which she handed to him. She watched as he put the pill into his mouth and drank the water down.

With care, he put the glass on the table by his bed, as she pulled the coverlet back and turned down the sheeted blanket. He was watching her as if in a trance.

She hesitated and her lips parted. He took her hand into his. They were facing each other. She almost smiled and she watched mesmerized as he took a step nearer.

He regarded her very seriously. His breathing was harsh. He carefully, gently took her into his arms and . . . he really kissed her!

She was thrillingly shocked and her nose drew in air as her mouth opened to his tongue. Her eyes widened in surprise as her body curled against his rigid one.

What on EARTH!

And his hunger grew. He really didn't let go of her as he discarded his jacket and stepped on the heels of his shoes to get rid of them. He was out of his sports shirt by dragging it off over his head and his trousers were no problem. Unzipped, they were peeled down . . . along with his underwear.

He was going to . . . ? She was shocked as she felt a strange fever build inside her body. Her breathing was odd. She looked at him and realized he was not in control of himself. But he was only positive. He wasn't hurting her. He was just very determined. Yeah, he was. And she was . . . ?

She wanted him. It wasn't compassion for his present, awful circumstances. It was him. She wanted this man. How shocking.

Why had this never happened before now? The two times she'd been involved with some man, it hadn't been this way. It had been rather abrupt and messy.

Why this man?

By then, he'd taken her dress off over her head and her slip straps were down her arms. Her bare chest was tightly pressed against the hair on his chest and it felt...marvelous. She gasped. But she pressed against him.

He growled in a guttural voice, "So you want me."

And pressing her round breasts in a rubbing swirl against him, she moaned!

It was as if she was an entirely different person. How could this be? She wasn't this kind of a woman. She barely—well, that was obvious—she was bare. But she hardly knew the—

Her back was on the bed. He moved her knees as he looked down her, and he lowered himself into her cradle.

He was very good but he was quick. It just so happened that she was triggered and it was an explosion of passion! Not of love but of body hunger. Passion.

No, it was release. Surcease.

How incredible.

And she knew she was at best a distraction. A substitute. A brief replacement. It wasn't she who was the recipient of his frantic, denying love.

With the emotional storm past, he dragged from her limp body and fell to the side of her. And he was out cold.

Two

For such a careful woman, it was a shock to Jessica to get up from the bed and look back at the man who had escaped into deep, exhausted sleep. She looked at him. He had a beautiful body. Her hands lingered on him.

Hesitating, she gazed at him. Finally, she carefully straightened him enough so that she could gently cover his body with the sheet and blanket.

Her own body was outrageously pleased and satisfied and murmuring. How could a body be separate from the mind? Well, however that was done, she was witness to her body's obvious greed. She wanted to get back into his bed. How shocking!

Jess's *mind* could have handled Zach's maneuvers, but it had blinked out. Her body had just...taken over. It had gone along...for the...ride?

It had most certainly been a ride. Wow. His poor dead wife. She'd never have that lustful man again.

Ummmm. How nice it had been with Zachary Thomas! How marvelous her body felt from its coupling with his. In the several times in the last five years when she'd tried it, it had never been the same for her as it had been with Zach.

She'd thought the whole experience had been lied about. But it was all true. She'd just found that out. It really *was* magic! It was only an awkwardly managed coupling, but how amazing.

It had to be this one man.

She looked on him, sleeping soundly. He was really something. He was out cold and snoring, a nice, comforting little bubble of sound. Her mother had always told her that a man's snore was something to investigate.

Her mother had *never* meant for Jessica to find out in just this way. And it came to Jess that this might not have been the right time of the month for her to have been so recklessly careless.

Yeah. There in a stranger's hotel room, she rearranged her clothing and tidied her hair. She couldn't do much for the whisker burn. Although she looked for a face salve in the kit acquired in their shop, apparently whisker burn had never been a problem for men.

Jess rubbed her abraded face with some ice from the container so carefully filled by room service.

She looked at herself in the mirror. She could get out of the hotel. She could have—she *should* have left at six when she was supposed to leave. But they were shorthanded, and she'd agreed to spell Vera while she had dinner. What a rash decision for her to have made.

She wondered if the ghost of Zach's wife had watched them—and if she had understood his grief. Any woman married at least twelve years to such a man would have understood him. Jessica did and she'd known him a much too brief time.

Then she realized that if she had been known to Zach, he wouldn't have taken her. Now, that was a curious thing to consider. How could she be sure it was so? It was.

Jess discreetly left the hotel and walked toward her little house only four blocks away. There was an old, pin oak tree, which dominated the entire yard. But the pecan trees found the shade nice.

The house was hers. She'd paid for it when her red-headed, great-grandmother had left Jess her fortune. Being the person she was, Jess had split the money with her two surviving siblings. One of her brothers had died.

Jess's little house was wood and painted white. It was a one-story frame house with roof peaks, and it sat on a corner. It was perfect for a single woman.

The porch curled around the house so that someone in a rocker could move to sit in the sun in winter and in the shade in summer. There were roses. Winter roses. TEXAS can be counter to the rest of the country. It's where the sun spends the winter.

Any number of women had sought to share Jessica's house. And it would have been noisy and fun to have had housemates living with her, but Jessica liked being alone in such a small, friendly town.

As Jess went up her walk, the cat was sitting on the porch with his tail curled around him in a patient manner. He gave her a growly smothered sound just like any male who is irritated with his slave being late to get home and therefore late in fixing his supper.

But the first thing Jessica did was go to her bedroom to check her calendar. She did it even before The Grouch got his supper. He mentioned her oversight in a rude yowl.

Jessica didn't hear him. It had been a long time since she'd needed to check on—the time of the month. She pushed up her bottom lip and considered how close she was to being vulnerable with that man. She stood a while in deep thought.

The cat's irritated yowl finally reached into Jessica's mind. And Jess went to find the cat food. She was thoughtful and had only tea as she sat distracted at the kitchen table.

She went to bed early. The cat got up on the bed and licked and licked and licked. She asked it, "What did you do all day that you didn't get a bath and have to do it all now?"

The cat lifted his head and speared her with an indignant look for long enough, then he discarded her and went back to licking.

Jess went to sleep.

She wakened the next morning as if she'd run the marathon—twice. She frowned at the cat in the middle of her bed and said, "If you can't share the bed, you'll have to sleep outside. Do you understand?"

The cat stretched and turned over to lie on his back. That was his invitation for her to spend time rubbing his fur and talking sweetly to him.

She did neither.

So the cat got down from the bed and stretched all different ways, as if sleeping with her had cramped his space, and then he went out to the kitchen to see if the mice had left anything on his plate.

The plate was pristine. Jess had begun to clean his plate because the mice liked cat food. He blinked with slow patience and waited.

The cat's slave hurried around and made her own breakfast and skipped the coffee after the first sip. That she couldn't drink the coffee caused her to thoughtfully sit at the table for some long time, looking out of the window and indifferent to the charming mews the cat managed to fake.

When she continued to ignore him, he went over and yowled at her. It was not a nice expression, but he was hungry, and she wasn't doing her duty to him.

Coldly, she looked at the cat and replied, "You could waddle around the house and catch a mouse or two."

He stalked across the kitchen floor, out the cat door and caught a lizard in about ten minutes. He didn't yowl the hunt cry but left the lizard's feet and head on the porch. Then he went down the alley to see what else was available.

It was a pensive day for Jessica. She didn't have the flu. She remembered her sister Alice throwing up the morning after her husband went to the Carolinas before going to the Middle East.

Alice's air force husband, Phil, had flown in, and said nothing to her of the reason for the surprise visit. It was allegedly a practice takeoff and landing trip. But he'd called her. She'd met him, they'd made love in her car, on the road just outside the airport. And the next day, Alice *knew* she was pregnant. Everyone else had scoffed. Even Phil when Alice told him. But she was and she'd known the next day.

Jessica's face softened. Was *she?*

She had a slow glass of milk and nothing else. Then she dressed in a distracted manner and walked indolently to the hotel. She wasn't too sharp that morning.

But during that day, Jess knew exactly what Zachary Thomas was doing. She had a nurse she chatted with at the hospital. In the late afternoon, Jess called her. "How is Mr. Thomas?"

"He saw the boy before the harvesters took what they could. This is a tough time for Mr. Thomas. He's at the funeral home sitting with his wife. Poor guy."

The boy's casket would be sealed.

Jess closed her books and told the manager, "I'm leaving early."

And he replied, "Ummm," without looking up.

So Jessica went over to the funeral home. And Zach was sitting in a chair near the open casket. He was deep in thought and didn't actually hear Jessica sit down next to him.

He looked at her.

She said, "This is tough. I'm sorry you have such a burden of grief so far from home. Being alone at this time must be especially sad for you."

His eyes were very serious. "I know what I did to you last night. I have no explanation for it. I apologize. Are you all right?"

"Of course."

"I've told Hannah."

"She'll understand."

"This has been such a nightmare. You gave me peace last night. I can't understand my doing something like that to a stranger. To you." He looked at Jessica and his eyes were troubled but clear. "I'm sorry."

"It's okay."

He sighed and looked away as he told her, "They're harvesting. The minister was here for some time. I really don't need anyone."

She started to move to leave.

"Please stay."

She sat back and was silent.

Then he asked her, "How will I get through all this without sealing it away in an emotional pus-like boil."

She nodded. "That about describes grief. It could possibly help you to write it all down, how it happened, and put in your feelings and emotions. It could help you to face it all.

"A lot of people can't communicate grief. You might sell such a sharing book. But if you never sell such a story, it's okay. You will have dealt with the whole shebang, and it's best to do it now."

"She went so gently."

So it was his wife for whom he grieved.

Thoughtfully, Zach added, "She was a good woman."

Jessica replied, "She'll make somebody a good guardian angel."

"She'll be looking after Mike."

Jess agreed, "Probably. For a while. He may want to explore."

Zach nodded. "Since he was taken, it is a comfort that she'll be with him."

That made Jess frown a little. The boy had to have been—what—eleven? Maybe twelve? Was that old enough to take care of himself? To distract her own self, Jess asked Zach, "What do you do for a living?"

"I'm a teacher."

He should be reasonably solvent. She waited.

Then Zach told her, "We came on this trip together because I'm not at home much. This was to get me better acquainted with Mike." Again Zach was silent before he asked, "Isn't that ironic? Now I'll never know him. But Hannah did. She was with him. She's still with him."

It was clear to Jessica that Zach was not especially good father material. If she really was pregnant with his baby, she'd go it all alone. She had no need to disrupt his life.

Well, from what he said, he hadn't disrupted his life for a wife or child. He'd lived his life his way—and on his own.

She was somewhat surprised he was sitting next to his neglected wife so uselessly. She was dead. What good was he now? She'd needed attention from him when she was alive.

Jessica started to rise, and Zach rose with her. "Would you walk with me on the beach? Yesterday's walk saved my sanity. I'm having a hard time assimilating the fact that I'm—alone."

She looked at him quickly, but he was looking at the waxen face of his wife.

So he did grieve. Perhaps if he'd realized nothing in life is for sure, he might have made a better husband.

If she *was* pregnant with his child, she absolutely would raise it alone. He was useless.

But he was a human being. One who was in grief. Belatedly, he was aware of his loss.

She asked, "Are there any arrangements you need to make?"

"The hospital and the minister both advised and guided me on those needs. They are professionals. And they were very kind. It's helped me."

She thought he might be a little self-centered. Well, maybe not. Nobody could do anything to help his late wife and son. They were gone.

But the son's contribution to the parts harvest had been allowed by the grieving father.

As if clued in by her thoughts, Zach just started in on speaking about his own thoughts. "Hannah would have loved helping others."

Jess figured Hannah worked in charities.

Zach admitted, "I'm new to the word 'harvest.' We were too late for her to help anybody. That would irritate her... not being able to help somebody else. I don't remember ever discussing what we should do—in case."

"Most of us feel we will live forever."

By then, they were out of the chapel and walking along the sidewalk toward the beach.

Zach mentioned, "We'll take the early plane home."

"Yes." She glanced over at him. He'd included his wife and son.

He was watching her, but as she looked at him, he looked away. He asked her, "Do you like your job?"

She grinned. "I'm brilliant with numbers." Then she added logically, "Keeping books is very satisfying to me."

He shook his head in rejection. "If bookkeeping is exciting for you, I'll send you all my income tax material and you can sort it out. That would be to show my gratitude for your—company—yesterday...and today. We are to leave tomorrow morning. They suggested that. They said it would be better to fly tomorrow. We'll be home by noon."

"I hope your life goes well."

He watched her. "And yours."

"Thank you."

How odd that Jess drove to the airport early the next morning. She just sat in her car at the parking lot. The hospital airport was a shuttle port. He'd go to Corpus or San Antone or even Houston to connect with another plane to go...home.

She would never see him again. She hadn't even asked for his address. It had been difficult for her to refrain from doing so. A part of her wanted a link.

From where she sat in her car, she watched the airplane lift and fly away. He was gone. She would never see him again.

Jess was then aware her hands were moving gently on her stomach to comfort the half orphan. The poor little beginning embryo.

What nonsense!

But she drove slowly from the airfield's parking lot and then drove along the highway to an isolated spot along the coast. She sat and watched the water and the sky.

There was no other place that matched the places in TEXAS. She was soothed by the panorama of subtle colors and the permanence of the Gulf.

Could she actually be pregnant? Or was her body just being difficult? Wanting a man. Wanting a *child?*

How could such a brief meeting make her body take up this weird conduct? It was hormones and the yearning of some strange part of her psyche. That way her orderly mind could excuse this idiocy.

But why on earth would her body want to fool her that way? Or was it she who was fooling her body?

Too many experts think humans are one entity. Their brains/bodies/subconsciouses have never debated an issue? We are more complicated than we will ever understand.

In such a time, think how Zach had turned to her with only using her body. He hadn't even *thought* about her as a person. Only a part of his mind remembered he'd taken her. He hadn't lusted for her. It had been a chance act. A really stupid one.

Why hadn't she resisted?

At the end of that day, she went home and slept in a drooling exhaustion. How could she be exhausted? She'd not done anything to be so zapped. She was grieving for a man with whom she'd had such a chance encounter?

Fiddlesticks.

Yes. Fiddlesticks. Her grandmother had used that word. It was better than the current shocking ones used in exasperation.

What had she done to 'exhaust' herself?

Nothing.

Jessica did the prerequisite chores and fed the offended cat. She walked the four blocks to the hotel to throw off the doldrums of her puzzling inertia.

In the middle of the morning, instead of tea, she had a glass of milk. Her stomach refused tea and she couldn't stand to smell the coffee. She picked at lunch. She had tomato soup for supper, with crackers and a glass of milk.

* * *

Just under two weeks later, Jess skipped her period. She decided it was spring fever, and she wasn't exercising nearly enough. She went out to jog and her breasts and stomach declined doing that.

She walked quite a distance. Not as far as she generally walked, but she had to sit down and rest before starting back.

It was the having-to-rest part that just about convinced Jess something was different. She'd ignored all the other signals.

She was quiet and thoughtful. Her work did not suffer. In that element of her life, she was brilliant as usual. But she canceled attending evening gatherings. She went to bed early. She slept like a log. Out cold. No awareness.

Zach called her in a month. He asked in a husky voice, "Are you okay?"

Toplofty, she replied, "Of course. Are you?"

He replied, "It's strange to go into a silent house."

Another week went by and nothing changed. Well, some things stayed changed. Jessica could tell something was going on. Her breasts were fuller. She continued to be picky with food. She finally went to a doctor... in Corpus. She was, indeed, pregnant.

She drove back to Sea View slowly and in some acknowledged shock. How could she do this to a child? Life was rough enough as it was. How could she face her parents? They'd be embarrassed and loyal.

Her sister Alice would be avidly curious. A *stranger?* How could Jess give in to a stranger! Miss Goody-Two-Shoes dallying with a *stranger? Who was it!*

Even the doctor had asked her that one. He was young, pleasant looking and interested. If she would for someone else, why not for him?

Being pregnant in Sea View's intimate, gossipy limitation was not going to be easy. How strange that she didn't even consider canceling the baby. Why not?

She wasn't sure why not. Being pregnant really wasn't real to her. She had to assimilate the fact first. Then she considered her situation.

She was self-supporting. No one had to donate to her health and welfare. She was on her own and could manage.

It would be rough on her family. They would be supportive and loyal, but it would be rough for them. And for her.

Would she find out Zach's address and let him know?

No.

Why burden him with such a problem?

He was the father. It might help him over this terrible time of being alone.

Actually, the fatal trip had been to bond him with his son. He hadn't been much of a part of his other family. Why would he be interested in sharing a surprise child?

He ought to be told.

She'd figure that out another time. He could get a DNA test and see how careless he'd been. *He* was—careless? What had *she* been doing in his room?

Don could have gone up with Zach. Actually, no one needed to go up with him. He was an adult. He could have handled himself. He *was* handling himself. She'd just gone along with him and been available.

A woman accompanying a man to a hotel room isn't all that smart. Some conduct is necessary for a woman under all circumstances. As her mother had always told her: *If you don't walk on the tracks, you won't get hit by the train!*

It was good advice.

So. She was just as responsible. She hadn't made one protest. Instead, she'd gone with him and sorted out his problems and even given him the pill so that he could sleep.

She had given more than a pill. She had given herself.

Had being twenty-nine triggered her foolish behavior? What would this do to the town? To her place in the town? To her family? To her? To the child? Yes, the child.

It was a little late for such thoughts. She ought to have figured it out sooner.

It was three months later, on a Friday morning, and Jessica had gone to the hotel. She was girding up to face the family's doctor, when who should walk into The Horizon but Zachary Thomas!

Him!

For some strange reason, she'd taken her eyes from the computer monitor. She looked through the open door past the desk as he approached the door and came through it.

He was more alert.

That was an interesting observation for her to have. She'd not thought, there he was, or what was he doing there, but that he was alert.

He looked wonderful! He was a really well-set-up human male animal. Her shocking body noticed. Her knees became subtly restless. Her breathing changed. Her eyes were enormous.

As he approached the desk, he looked through the door and saw her. He grinned and kept his eyes on Jessica.

When Don came to the desk, Zach shook his head and grinned as he continued to look at Jess. He lifted his chin and said, "I've come to see Jessica Channing."

Her lips suddenly puffy and parting, Jess pushed back her swivel chair and walked to the desk's counter like an uncontrolled robot.

He didn't say hello or anything normal; he asked, "Are you free?"

She could have replied in any number of ways, but she nodded.

He said, "Come walk on the beach with me."

It was raining. It was a nice early summer's rain. She put on her raincoat because Don held it for her. As she walked around the end of the counter, Don gave Zach an umbrella.

The two walkers didn't say anything. They just went out of The Horizon and down onto the beach. Zach was in very casual clothing. He'd just gotten off a shuttle plane. He was there.

Jess looked at him now and again. His face was relaxed. His eye crinkles crinkled as he smiled down at her. He breathed deeply and sighed in contentment.

In three months, he was back to see another woman? That was quick.

He said, "Some of the recipients of the Donor Harvest are coming to the hospital tomorrow. I was invited to meet them. This was an opportunity to see if you are real. You are."

Grieving for his wife, he'd noticed another woman?

She looked at the TEXAS sky, which was in shades of gray. It was beautiful. The rain was misty and touched her hot face. Her metabolism had changed and she was generally too warm.

He said, "You've lost some weight. You're skinny. Are you all right? Your cheeks are hot. Are you well?"

She replied, "Yes." That was for whatever he'd said. She didn't mention that the skinniness wouldn't last.

As they went back toward the hotel, he asked awkwardly, "Could you take the afternoon off and... be with me? Tomorrow would you go with me? I'm not sure... how to handle... all this. You were so logical last time. I will never be able to repay you for your help."

She blushed scarlet just about all over, but he saw her face redden. He was startled. "Are you all right?"

She assured him, "Yes."

His hand caught hers. "I'm glad. You were such a help to me. You were so calm. I don't think I could ever make it up to you. If you should ever need any kind of help, I'd be grateful if you'll let me be the one, or at least be in the crowd that would help you."

She looked down at her feet while she could still see them. Pregnant women said such. But she again blushed scarlet. Damn!

In some earnestness, Zach pressed, "Are you okay? Why did you blush that way?"

"It's nothing." *Nothing!*

He took her arm and stopped her steps. "Jessica, you wouldn't hide from me, would you? You and Paul could claim my very life in support. You both have calls on me. If there is *any*thing—"

"There isn't."

He watched her soberly. And she looked everywhere else.

Zach asked gently, "Will you go with me to the hospital?"

She looked down but she said, "Yes."

"I have a strong feeling you'd rather not go with me, but I accept that you will go along and I'll hold you to the agreement."

She nodded.

He shortened his steps as he looked at his watch. And he pretended to be offhand as he closely quizzed her. "Everything at the hotel okay?"

"Yes."

"Your family all okay?"

He wasn't one damned bit subtle. He knew something was riding her. Well, something had ridden her. Him. How was she to get through this? Would she have to get rid of him again? Get on with it all alone?

He was down to asking, "The town's steady?"

And somewhat irritated, she replied to him, "No earthquakes, either."

So he was silent. As they walked, he turned his head and looked around as men do, but he was thinking and his eyes squinted just a bit.

Finally, he asked, "Are you involved with some man?"

"Not seriously."

Zach stopped and demanded, "But you admit you are involved?"

And she was honest. "In a manner of speaking, I . . . was."

He said nothing.

She looked up at Zach and there he was, good-looking, serious, interested, concerned. Hell.

Softening his male voice, he told her, "If you have any problem, at all, tell me how to help you. I owe you."

She replied briefly, "No."

Three

Jessica took Zachary to her parents' house for lunch. She hadn't even called them ahead of time. The two just went there. She introduced him as Zach Thomas. And she named her parents as Mark and Cynthia Channing.

Jess's red hair, green eyes and translucent skin were her mother's. Cynthia was a beauty. And it was easy for Zach to say, "I know what a beauty Jessica will be in her time."

How many times had Cynthia heard such talk about her precious daughter? It was a given. How can one take credit for something over which one has no input? Cynthia barely smiled. But her green eyes weighed what sort of man Zachary Thomas might be.

That made Zach smile.

Cynthia said to him, "I remember you. Paul Butler was so concerned for you."

"I would never have made it, if Paul and Jessica hadn't been there."

Her parents nodded once to acknowledge his words.

Mark Channing ran Sea View's weekly newspaper and was always home for lunch. Well, on some Thursdays when the paper was being put to bed, Cynthia took her husband's lunch and sometimes his supper to him.

Jessica's parents welcomed Zach and made him comfortable with their casual TEXAS manners. And with skillful subtleness her mother added enough of everything in sandwiches and salad to include the surprise guest quite easily. She was used to doing that.

It was natural ... seeming. Both parents were ordinarily very curious. However, the only really comfortable person there was Zach. Both parents' eyes caught every minute as Zach's glances lighted on their daughter.

Jessica's cheeks were scarlet. She licked her lips a lot. She held herself calmly in check.

And the parents looked at Zach. They narrowed their eyes and listened to him. He was talking about teaching. Then he touched on witnessing the harvest results the next day.

Vulnerably, he said, "I'm not sure I can handle seeing kids who have transplants from Mike. Jess has been kind enough to agree to go with me. She and Paul Butler have been so supportive. I don't know what I would have done without them."

Zach's face was so calmly earnest.

The parents watched silently.

Jessica toyed with her food and her cheeks continued scarlet.

The conversation gaps didn't bother Zach. Jessie's dad said enough and her mother's observations were neutral as usual. She never had appeared to be strident, but Jess knew her to be ironhanded adamant.

Jess wondered when her mother would quit silently considering her and begin to question her. Right then, her mother was considering—Zach. She was a courteous, well-brought-up woman who was now reserved.

Jessica sighed without seeming to. She had learned to do that in her early years. It was of special need for their aging preacher's rambling sermons.

When would Jessica Channing get a sermon from their next relatively new, but now aging preacher? Who would tell him that Jessica Channing was pregnant?

Not her parents. She could get to nine and a half months and her parents wouldn't publicly "notice" any difference in her unless she mentioned it to them.

At the table, next to Jess, was the father of her child. And although Zach was sensitive enough to realize that there was something bothering her, it hadn't occurred to him that *he* was a part of it.

Should she tell him?

Ah, how could she? He was now so free! Actually, he'd probably been this markedly individual all of his life. He was on his own. He had been that way even with a family to support. And the deaths of Hannah and Mike had shocked him raw. But now he was getting back to being himself.

Jess wondered if Zach had ever worried about either his wife or his son in the years he'd been a part of their lives. Had he just turned all domestic problems over to Hannah? He'd felt filled with just worrying about his students and left the rest of their lives to Hannah?

That sounded probable.

Zach could delegate worry. He would take care of the students he had under his supervision, and Hannah would have had the responsibility of Mike and the household. It would have been she who had the worry of Mike. Mike and the furnace. Add the garbage disposal and the repairs on the car. Hannah would have done all of those things. She'd probably been a gem of a woman.

But Hannah had escaped.

Escaped?

Well. There had been that "at peace" expression on Hannah's shell. In her coffin, she'd looked like any woman who had successfully completed the spring cleaning...early.

Hannah had probably been the perfect mate for Zachary Thomas. Jessica looked critically at Zach, who was explaining something to her parents. They were listening.

Whatever he was explaining, it was probably about school and students. He was too aloof to get down to the nitty-gritty of actual, everyday living.

Zach knew she was in some kind of trouble. If he knew that she was pregnant, he would assume it was because of some other man. His sperm wouldn't be so crass as to impregnate an unsuitable woman. Unsuitable in that she was not married to him.

He would never leave strings loose and not neatly tied. Well, he never had before. Never knowingly.

When a month was up, he had called her and asked. And at that time, she had denied any problem.

* * *

It was quite a while after lunch before the pair pushed back their chairs. They helped her parents to clear off the table and stack things in the dishwasher. Then Zach surprised Jess. He did an excellent job of sweeping the kitchen floor. Generally, only TEXANS know to carefully sweep a floor so as not to leave any morsel to tempt cockroaches and mice.

With that jewel of a wife, when had Zach learned to sweep a floor? He'd probably just lifted his feet. He'd probably learned by watching as she'd done it.

It was some time later that the ill-assorted pair took their leave from Jess's parents and walked down toward the very center of town. It was still raining gently. She wore the raincoat and he handled sharing the umbrella.

Of course, people called and honked as is done in a small town. And Jessica waved and on occasion called back.

It was Paul Butler who altered his route and walked to them. He wore a Stetson and a raincoat. He shook hands with Zach and nodded to Jess. Then, he asked Zach, "Is there anything I can do for you?"

How typical of the man to ask.

Zach replied easily, "Jess has promised to go along. Let me thank you again for your support at that time, three months ago... and the offer now."

Paul nodded soberly, but he then looked over at Jessica. "You okay?"

"Yes." She lifted her chin a single notch and was pleasant.

Paul considered her. "You look a little flushed." He was blunt.

Looking at Jessica with a frown, Zach joined that conversation. "I asked her. She almost looks sunburned. But it's mostly just her cheeks." He added just to Paul, "She gets a little cross if you pry too much."

The words only proved Zach didn't know.

Paul considered. Then he said to Jess, "If ever you need help, I'm here."

That made Zach very alert. For a man like Paul to offer help, there must be an obvious need of help. Zach forgot Paul and turned to Jessica. "Are you okay?"

And she slid a killing glance across to Paul as she confronted Zach with honest eyes to reply, "Of course. There is no problem."

Paul replied in a very ordinary voice, "If ever there is, you know where I am."

Zach was still centered on Jess and his attention was riveted. "And me." He was intense. "You do know how to get in touch with me if you need help?"

Unnoticed, forgotten, Paul left them.

Zach got out his wallet and found a card, which he handed to Jessica. "Put it somewhere that you will remember. Call me before you call anyone else. I owe you."

While Jessica did take the card and put it in her pocket, she tried to continue down the street, but Zach stopped her by taking her arm in his hand. He was very earnest. "Why did Paul say that to you? Are you in some kind of trouble?"

"Of course not! If I was, I have parents, a sister, a brother, uncles, aunts, cousins, the whole, entire damned town!" She was a little strident.

Zach was startled and he straightened as he frowned. "Jess . . . what is all this?"

And in a very deadly serious voice, she replied, "Nothing."

Not speaking, they then went on down the sidewalk to the beach. The silence continued. He glanced at Jessica, but she did not look at him even once.

They didn't walk on the beach, they strolled. Jessica could walk her usual distance again. The exercise was important, she knew. And with the jitters of Zach's arrival, she could have walked miles. The baby wouldn't mind. Her body was becoming invigorated.

She wondered if her inertia in the first months was to allow the baby time to adjust to living. Or was it to help her own body to alter and nurture? When she finally got up the nerve to admit being pregnant to her local doctor, she would ask.

Maybe. She might just go and be examined and be surprised. Shocked? It would be easy to be shocked. She already was.

Then she looked over at Zach. Why in this world would he have had to contact her so openly—now—when she was hoping the town had forgotten him? If he hadn't come back and come to her at the hotel, the town wouldn't have thought of them as being a pair.

He'd expanded the whole idea by coming to the hotel and taking her out of it . . . in the rain! No subtle man takes a woman out walking in the rain. TEXAS men don't notice the rain, or they are so exuberant over it that they feel they ought not block the moisture from the ground, so they stay inside the house, or the car or their trusty truck.

She glanced over at Zach. He would walk in the rain with a strange woman in a small town. It wouldn't occur to him to be subtle. He was a teacher but he didn't teach tact. What *did* he teach? She wouldn't ask. He might think she was interested in him.

At that minute, Zach asked Jess, "What are you feeding me for supper?"

She turned her head slowly and just stared at him in shock. He was inviting himself to her house for dinner? She dismissed such a foolish thing. "I just have peanut butter on Friday night."

"Good. You have no idea of all the casseroles I've been getting from the single women up north. I believe there are even women from Ohio who bring the casseroles over to Indiana. No, don't scoff!" He held up his free hand as he shook his head.

She hadn't said a word or even looked at him until then. She frowned in temper. Her temper was getting quick over nothing . . . just lately.

Zach went on, "I like peanut butter. It's a good basic food. My mother allowed it. I would be pleased to share your peanut butter with you this evening, Miss Channing."

Belligerently hostile, she retorted, "You may not spend the night at my house!"

He appeared shocked. "Of course not. Even I know better than that!"

"I should hope so!"

He smiled so tenderly. "That night you were so sweet to me. I've never had such a partner! You squirmed under me and your hands were in my hair and down pressing my butt. You made the most sexual sounds I've ever heard. You wiggled and—"

"I did not!"

He laughed. "I haven't had but three women in all my life, and Hannah was very sweet. But, Jessica Channing, you—were—wild! You shocked this innocent."

"You are hardly an innocent."

"It took me a month of pacing before I could think of another reason to call you. Hannah was a good woman. I miss her. She was such an efficient wife. She had control on all problems. And she was sweet to lov—"

"I don't want to hear it!"

But he didn't hush up. He told her positively, "While she was sweet, you're a shock!"

Jessica drew in an unexpellable breath and retorted indignantly, "I am nothing of the sort!"

He didn't reply, but he smiled such a closemouth, delighted smile and his eyes danced wickedly.

In a very deadly voice, she told him, "Hannah and—Mike—are only just . . . in their graves."

Zach replied with candor, "It seems so much longer than that. I miss them."

"Not much."

He shook his head and said it sincerely. "I miss them every day."

"But you can still talk sex to me?"

He was startled. Genuinely surprised. "I miss them. You're another problem altogether. A separate, difficult, remarkable problem."

"In *three* months?"

He smiled tenderly. "I've counted the time, too. It seems longer since we were together, doesn't it?"

"She would have a fit if she knew you were talking this way to me, this soon."

He seriously studied her words. He pushed up his lower lip and shook his head slowly before he said, "No. She was different. She wasn't at all possessive. She laughed so gently when students—that is, girls— got a crush on me. She was a tolerant woman."

"I believe you only see and know what you want to see and know."

And he considered that additional premise. Then he nodded and said, "That could well be. But I've never experienced anything like we had that one time."

"You weren't even really cognizant. You were a walking zombie."

He agreed. "And you took advantage of me by tipping my fragile body over onto the bed and having your wicked way with a helpless man."

She gasped in shock!

And he was so crass that he laughed in delight.

Her eyes narrowed. "You're teasing me."

He replied with a grin, "It's one way to get your attention."

"I have had enough attention and—"

He shook his head and put his arms out to fall back to his sides. "I'll just bet you have!"

She went on in a very positive manner. "I don't need yours at this time. You are foolish to keep me to yourself in a town this size."

He smiled faintly as he looked around. "This is a good town."

"Yes. Don't get me ostracized by paying this much attention to me. People take note."

He protested quite readily, "I'm only here for the weekend."

She reminded him with a sober tone, "I live here."

He watched his feet, then he considered her. His words then were serious. "I understand."

"What do you mean . . . you understand?"

"I've rented a car. We can sneak out of town."

"No."

He smiled. "Okay."

"What's that mean?"

He shrugged. "You're in charge. I'll do whatever pleases you."

"Pleases . . . me?"

He laughed. "You're a wild and woolly woman. I'll do whatever you say."

"Stay away from me."

He instantly protested, "Now, Jess, you've invited me to supper and—"

"You invited yourself!"

"Was I that smart?" He grinned. Then, he said with pleased humor, "I'm improving. I hadn't known how to do anything like that. I must be getting smarter."

By then they were on her porch. The cat was there, looking superiorly patient.

Observing the cat, Zach commented as he nodded, "So. A cat owns you."

She opened the unlocked door as she said, "You know cats."

"I've escaped, so far."

The cat got into the house first. It was such a gloomy day that Jessica turned on the living room lamp. She took off her raincoat and hung it on the porch. She opened the hotel's just-closed umbrella and put it on the floor of the porch behind the swing. She did it so that the umbrella wouldn't be blown away. The wind was getting gusty.

Standing there, watching her, he said in some astonishment, "You don't have to lock your doors."

"Not yet."

He opened the door again and then followed her inside. "I don't like it that you don't lock your doors."

"Tough."

Zachary observed Jessica and scolded with some chiding, "You've gotten sassy since I saw you last. Where is the compassionate woman I knew then?"

"Gone."

His grin widened considerably. "I think I like this one better."

"Don't be a fool."

He smiled at her without a reply. Then he went into the kitchen and washed his hands.

He had the cheek to open her refrigerator and even went into the freezer. He took potatoes from the drawer in the refrigerator. He scrubbed two, pierced them and put them into the oven.

Looking farther, he found a steak to share. And by hunting, he found the readily available lettuce, onions, tomatoes and croutons for a salad.

A little grouchy and feeling put-upon, she watched him silently.

He would catch her rejecting glance and smile at her. Then he had the gall to suggest, "You could set the table."

Her house, her food, and he allowed her to set the table?

She set the table.

He trimmed the fat off the sides of the steak, chopped it into very small pieces and gave them to the cat.

Jessica was patient. "Cats aren't supposed to eat fat."

"Today is a special day. We eat what we want. I only gave him a little of the actual meat. If you'll notice, I chopped it up and mixed it into his nutritional junk."

How could a woman spurn a man who was so tolerant? Who didn't understand rejection? Who was the actual person, Zachary Thomas? She'd have to try harder.

It was impossible for her to call some of her friends and have them come to her house as chaperones. They would be too curious and never let up on the questions. They would think he was charming and complete. With just the two of them there, she could hardly lose her virginity. She carried his child.

At this time, he must not know about the baby. Such a revelation was too soon for him. How could she lure him into commitment at a time like this? What would all the people in his hometown think? For a teacher, that would matter.

She watched him, sternly cautioning her body to behave. While she didn't remember being the "wild" he claimed, she did remember that she'd—participated.

Well, she could very well have—submitted. She'd probably been—involved. She could have had her hands on him. She might have even—helped.

It had been . . . wonderful.

She slid her eyes discreetly down his body. It could happen again. One more time. She could lie with him and experience that wonderful, remarkable thrilling coupling.

Coupling.

Two together and coupled.

Her body yearned. Her breasts got pushy. When had her breasts been pushy! The last time she'd been with him. The only time such pushiness had ever happened. She had been ... outrageous.

She could be again.

He would leave. With her already being three months pregnant, no one in the town would consider he was the father when she became obvious.

This was a fluke. Actually, he was in Sea View for only one reason: to witness the fact the harvest had worked. Such a gathering would probably never happen again. Now was the time to experience him one more time. A last time.

She would.

How could she begin?

She couldn't instantly turn from being vinegar into being honey. She had to be subtle or he might smell a mouse. A greedy female rat? *She* would use *him* this time. He was mature enough to handle being used.

He found the wine. Good. Candy's dandy but liquor's quicker.

She offhandedly declined any.

He hesitated. "Are you sure? There's enough for both of us."

"No. Not tonight."

He grinned. "You're thinking I'll try to seduce you?"

And instead of snubbing him, she allowed herself a small smile. But she also blushed. Well, hell, she did that over nothing. It was her "condition" which caused that to happen.

He tilted his head as he considered her. "I just might seduce you. I'm trying to keep my hands off you. You would be amazed at my restraint."

Well, damn. Restraint? Now, how was she to combat restraint? She allowed her lashes to close down as she considered.

He said in a husky voice, "You ought to be careful of me. You tempt me."

Her eyes popped open and she looked with amazed delight at him. She'd tempted him? How?

He said, "There you go again. That was worse. Better. Unfair." He looked at her from under his eyebrows and he smiled just a bit.

She was unfair? He did that unfairly! He was just asking for it. This time, she would seduce him. She watched him. And he watched back.

He said, "Shall I tussle you around now? Would you like me to put the steak back in the refrigerator?"

Who ever used the whole word? He was a teacher. He said words correctly.

He went on in a sly, casual manner, "Or would you like to do a revamp of the dinner scene in *Tom Jones?*"

"I do remember that scene." She again smiled just a tad but standing still and seemingly demure she watched him with intently disturbing hunger. In the film, the hero and a woman watched each other avidly as they ate their meal salaciously.

Just his watching her was an aphrodisiac. He put his hands in his trouser pockets. His grin was wider. "Which do you choose?"

Her eyes closed down almost halfway, and she smiled again.

He leaned his head back as he gasped out loud. "Woman! Be careful how you rattle this poor and lonely stranger."

He was mimicking Gary Cooper or one of those other early cowboys who had seemed basically mostly innocent with women.

Jess told him, "I'll fix the salad." Then she added in a snippy manner, "I like my share of the steak very well-done."

He looked at the meat, pushed his hands deep into his pants pockets and lifted his head to the ceiling. "I hope I survive this."

She smiled very kindly and told him with gentle assurance, "You will."

He scolded, "Telling me I'll survive your attack isn't any help at all! You ought to chat about the weather!"

So she said to him, "TEXAS springs are like this. It can go on for days."

He asked rather intently, "How soon do I have to be at the hotel—discreetly?"

She didn't even hesitate a discreet time. She replied right away, "Before eleven."

"There ought to be a list of the rules somewhere around. Do you have a copy?"

And she was wicked. "I'll instruct you as we go along."

The change in her attitude did catch his attention. It only made him careful not to rock the boat. His smile was humor, but his eyes were hot coals. His voice was gravelly as he told her, "I get a 'hello' kiss."

She turned her head and inquired with slightly raised eyebrows, "Do you mention it first?"

He wasn't stupid. He went to her in an almost careful swagger and took control of her with gentle possessiveness, and he really kissed her.

With their mouths glued together and her hands in his hair, he squeezed her to his body from top to bottom. His nose could handle his harsh breathing. She became a little faint.

It wasn't the kiss. It was her delicate condition. It wasn't being against him thataway, it was just that she didn't have enough oxygen. But she didn't wiggle or press her hands against him, asking to be released.

Her hands on his head were holding his face to hers. She was outrageous. And she *knew* she was. She was acting shamelessly greedy. And she knew that, too. But a woman doesn't often have the chance to experience a man like that for a second time.

And this time would take longer.

A little moan sounded in her throat.

He lifted his mouth as much as she allowed and asked, "You are okay?" His breaths were loud and rapid. His pupils were dilated. His nostrils were flared.

She smiled. She had all of his attentions.

Trembling, he asked, "Now?"

And she looked at him big-eyed and serious. "We have to eat. If we leave the kitchen now, it would appear we were not having supper on time."

He really didn't understand small towns, but he said, "Oh." That was a nothing reply that had no meaning at all to either of them.

Then he waited for any signal she might give. She could sneak him into the living room, or the bedroom, or just use the kitchen table.

She released him and took up the awesome butcher knife.

That did freeze him and his eyes were intent and serious.

She chopped off one-third of the steak. And she busily put her third into the heated skillet.

He blinked. Probably it was for the first time in several minutes. His eyes felt a little dry, so he blinked again.

She began to assemble the salad. He didn't say a word. He put his hands back into his pants pockets and moved slowly so that he was handy in case she wanted another kiss from him.

She looked up at him seriously, and they exchanged a very vibrant expression. Then she smiled a little. That made him restless. He twitched and moved a bit but he stayed close to her.

Four

Their dinner wasn't as rowdy as *Tom Jones*'s but it was similar. Jessica's lazy-eyed smile was a shiver down Zach's attentive sex. His presence across the table was a stimulation to hers. She watched his mouth.

His busy eyes watched whatever of her that he could see.

She breathed and her dress pulled on her breasts. Or maybe it was her breasts that tugged on her dress?

Whatever it was, it was distracting to him.

So was the way she chewed. How she glanced from her plate to his face. The hungry look was in her eyes. Was that true? She was hungry for him? She might devour him.

Okay. He could handle being devoured. And he shifted in his chair and cleared his throat. He wondered if ever before in all his adult life, he had ever been this stimulated. She stirred him. He couldn't organize his breathing and he felt like a neophyte.

She really wobbled him. Surely she'd do something about him. It wasn't as if he was a stranger to her. Of course, when they'd mated, shared, whatever it was they'd done, it had been quick.

He'd given her no chance to protest. He'd been emotionally fogged. She had just been there at that time. He'd needed release. She was in his room with him, and he'd acted on impulse.

They were just lucky she hadn't gotten caught.

He looked at her sitting across from him there at the table. Her back was straight and she was enjoying her food. She licked her lips in a nice, subtle, excessively sexual manner and took the bit from her fork. Subtly, she began to chew.

Now, that wasn't really as erotic as he was pretending. She was eating. That was all. She was hungry, and she was eating in a very ladylike manner. This was not *Tom Jones*.

Yeah, it was.

She was a lascivious woman. Her heavily lidded eyes glanced over to him in a lazy, seductive manner. She chewed in an alluring way, slowly and sexually...

How could chewing be sexual?

He weighed if she was sexy, and she sure as all hell was! She was driving him right up the wall. She had him on his ear! No. He was sitting on a chair at the table.

He looked at her critically. Then he suggested, "Unbutton your dress, uh, I think two buttons will do it." Then he smiled pleasantly, harmlessly and waited, breathing carefully as if calm.

She looked down at her pushy chest, then she lifted those big, green, bedroom eyes to his and replied, "My dress buttons are just fine the way they are."

He could argue that. He put down his fork and leaned back in his chair. He said, "No. If you will re-call *Tom Jones,* the lady with him was pushed up and just about over the top of her dre—gown."

She considered, looked at her tidy chest, then looked again at him as she said, "You're right."

He smiled and waited.

She took another bite, and again her glance came to his waiting face.

Obviously interested, he said, "Some problem?"

And she inquired, "About . . . what?"

He lifted his eyebrows a tad and explained with a slowly-moving-out hand to indicate his directions, "The spillover."

She looked again at her chest and then back at him. And her humor got to her. She smiled just a slight bit and squinched her eyes in chiding. But then she licked her lips and studied the food on her plate.

He said, "Please." His tone was one of practical logic. "Let's be more accurate."

She considered him and what she planned for him that evening. She shifted in her chair and looked at her covered chest. Then, by golly, she reached one hand to fiddle with the top button.

She heard his intake of breath, and she wondered if the last three months had been very barren for him. As barren as for her? Everyone had said that being preg-nant drove a woman sexually wild. It had to be some-thing about being pregnant and therefore...safe? She wanted his body almost desperately.

There was no other man around that she would ask to help her in this time. She was so sexually hot that she was sitting on that chair—and not astraddle Zach's lap—only because of her severe control.

She unbuttoned the top button. The material only relaxed a bit, but it didn't fall open. However, she felt like a cheerfully scarlet woman.

He said, "And the next one?"

That surprised her. She glanced at him and saw his hunger. She looked down at her chest and her smothered smile did curl the corners of her lips.

She licked them slowly before she tucked her lower lip into her mouth.

Then she lifted both hands and freed the second button.

With the weight of the material, the buttons parted a tad more.

His breathing picked up quite audibly. He didn't say one word. He was still trying to be casual.

Then he told her, "You're supposed to flirt."

Her surprised eyes came up to observe him. "Flirt?"

"Yeah."

"Like . . . what?"

"Even in a town this size, the women know to flirt. You've watched TV, you have to know something about life, men and sex."

"I watch the Learning Channel and PBS."

He was shocked. "You've avoided the other channels?"

She lifted a quieting hand and added, "CNN."

"You watch only three channels?" His voice was disbelieving.

"I just don't have much time for it. There is always so much to do."

She'd be that type.

But being a teacher, he never could just plow on in, he had to explore the premise and be sure he understood. "What all do you do?"

"Besides my work at the hotel, I am the victim of my friends. I baby-sit." She glanced up and gave him a waiting look as she discreetly licked her lips.

"Who does that to a single woman who is thirty ye—"

"Twenty-nine." She was calmly authentic and accurate.

"Twenty-nine years old?"

"That's why I put my raincoat and umbrella outside. It's the signal that I have a guest."

"Ahhhh. What do you do in summer?"

"I hang my bathing suit on the line."

"Clever." He nodded. How many men had she harbored, locked with her in this house, with their bodies being voraciously used?

She smiled just a little.

And his libido wondered avidly, why did she smile at that? Was it...memories? Was she mentally flipping through the files of names stacked in her libido? His eyes narrowed. She would. Where did he rank?

As fast as he'd taken her, back then on that horrific night, what would she remember? Not a whole lot. Zach should have been smooth and slow. If he had been aware enough to realize just what he was up to, he'd have had better sense. If he'd been working, then, on all cylinders, he wouldn't have taken her at all.

But he knew that Jessica had loved it. Zach had the scratches on his back for almost a week. They'd been her hungry, holding scratches on his back. She'd been trying to get him closer. They hadn't been scratches of rejection. She had wanted him very badly.

Zach smiled at his hostess, who was eating slowly and savoring her food. She had a good appetite. She needed to eat well. She was a little slender. Not quite skinny. Her breasts... Yeah. Each was a man's handful.

And his hands curled in the wanting.

With Jessica's movements, the opening of her blouse was widened. She reached discreetly to get the butter plate and took some before she put it in a place more convenient for him.

Stretching that way caused her blouse opening to become quite attention-getting. Then she turned her body to see if the cat had finished his supper. And the opening of her blouse widened farther.

His smile was very vulnerable as he considered her. He wasn't really aware that she was now watching him. He'd turned into mush. She wouldn't have any trouble luring him into bed. She looked at the clock. There was time.

How greedy of her.

Jessica's bottom was so hot that she had to move a little and her knees rubbed. She felt like Mae West during her remarkable interview with a very amused Edward R. Murrow.

Jessica asked, "Is there anything else you want?" And her face was so kind.

Zach said, "Yeah."

"Name it." She licked her lips.

And he replied, "You."

From the floor, the watching tomcat thought, *How eye-closingly silly. No imagination at all. Any witness would have groaned and been impatient. It didn't work that way with the two at the table—*

With that observation, the cat went out the cat door onto the porch. It is said that cats understand human speech. It's just that we aren't smart enough to grasp their basic try for communication with us.

So the cat had abandoned being witness to the boring, adolescent exchange. Who could learn conduct from humans? Think of a feline asking: *Is there anything else you want?* And a male replying: *Yeah!* And the feline saying: *Name it?* No male cat—well, he might.

But under such circumstances, any tom would wonder how the kits would turn out.

Not even knowing that the cat had left through the small cat door, the riveted man at the table was watching the woman. His eyes were avid and his body was very alert.

So was Jess's. She was not aware of her skill in sensuality. She could lick her lips in the slowest, most alluring manner. She raised her eyes in such lazy flirting.

But she was really only checking on him. She was so hot that she ought to have had a faint wisp of smoke rising from her hot body.

Zach felt like fanning around his own body—he was that hot. The smell of hot sex was actual. And his breathing was getting harsh; his lungs were in overdrive.

While Jess squirmed her bottom slightly in a mind-swamping manner, she seemed languid. She moved slowly. Moving her hand, lifting her eyelids, turning her head were all done with unknowing seductive movements.

Zach was riveted.

Jessica was only just beginning to breathe higher in her chest.

Men are just quicker than women.

It was a good thing that they weren't in a restaurant. The whole, entire place would have been a writhing mess of influenced people. Sex is catching.

He asked, "Are you through?"

And she wondered—with what?

He said, "Let's take our glasses into the living room."

She smiled a little and said, "All right." But then she got up and carried the plates to the sink to rinse and put them into the dishwasher.

Zach couldn't believe it. She was programmed to tidy up and she just went ahead and did it.

So he helped. It wasn't from any feeling of tidiness; he was bent on getting her on the sofa. Getting her into bed too fast might slow her down or make her argue.

He needed to get closer to her.

Cleverly, he blocked the cat's door. In the middle of something tense, they didn't need the damned cat jumping up to investigate what was going on. Nothing rivals a curious cat when a man is being earnest about a woman.

With the kitchen tidy—enough—they took their glasses to the living room. Hers of milk. His was wine.

What with one thing and another, Zach's breathing was harsh. She was aware of it. She asked, "Do you have a lung problem?"

He replied, "No." Short and sweet. Then he kissed her.

They were almost on the sofa. Her glass of milk tipped. Since her hands were under his arms and around to his back, some spots went onto his shirt back. That would be an interesting puzzle for any female laundry person. Why would he have drops of milk on the back of his shirt?

But she tilted the glass and only lost a little of the milk. She did kiss him back. She made a pleasured sound.

That was an aphrodisiac. By then, *any*thing she'd do would rouse him further. He was breathing through his open mouth. His body trembled in a shiver. He was intense.

She was like a female cat in heat. She made sounds and she moved slowly against him, rubbing him like a cat marking her territory. She wanted his attention.

She had it.

He was getting hyper. He told her, "I've thought about you."

That gave her a pause. She sobered and was serious.

"When they asked me if I would like to come down here, I remembered you and I wanted to see you again."

To her, that was better.

He said, "You are so special."

How many times had she heard that line? Actually, quite a few. It was the opening statement for men. Well, an opening.

He told her, "I love your hair. It smells good."

Her *hair* smelled good? That was an odd thing to say. So she washed her hair fairly often. If she didn't, it was greasy.

"Your green eyes are different. I don't know many green-eyed women. I've been looking at the kids at school and the other teachers and there aren't any who have green eyes that I've seen."

"I was lucky?"

"Absolutely."

She laughed in her throat. That, too, was an aphrodisiac. He held her closer to him, and she felt him tremble. His hunger for her aroused her. He really, really wanted her.

And she was willing.

It was he who said, "Let's go into the other room." That way, he didn't actually have to say the word *bed*. For this small-town woman, the word could set off her alarm bells.

Then he kissed her in a very earnest way. And she was aware that he wasn't overly skilled. But he was most certainly earnest.

So she allowed him to direct her, and she went along, testing what he would do and how he would go about it.

He asked, "In here?"

It was the guest room. To Jessica, that did seem to be appropriate.

He was already disrobing as he flipped back the coverlet and unzipped his trousers. He was quick. And he helped her with the buttons on her dress. His hands trembled so much that he fumbled. But the backs of his hands fumbled around her breasts.

Jess wondered if he was actually that awkward or was he groping deliberately? He was groping.

And she soon knew how deliberate it was. He moved the backs of his hands on her breasts. It was very erotic. Her chest loved it. So did the rest of her.

He cradled one breast in his hand as his other arm went about her, holding her close to him. And he kissed her better, more earnestly, with real skill.

When he raised his mouth to look at her in his arms, she said, "You've done this before."

He replied, "Yes."

"What's next?"

Being a good teacher, he explained with open candor, "I've got to get you out of that dress and whatever else you're wearing."

"You weren't that picky, not the last time."

He shook his head slowly as his unsteady hands finished unbuttoning her dress. "I only remember what a relief you were to me, and what a wonderful release it was. You helped me so much that night."

She couldn't think of anything to say in reply.

He told her with a slow shake of his head, "It was such a terrible day, and I was a far way out from normal. I was just about desperate inside of myself. How had all that happened? I'd had no control over any of it. I couldn't change anything or even prevent it. What was next? How could I live? Why us? I was in a maelstrom of despair. I couldn't cope. You gave me peace. Escape."

And guess what he had given her!

He said, "I didn't mean to turn this into a soul-pouring spewing of what had happened. This is now. I want you. You are so sweet. You feel so good against me. Kiss me. Kiss me and let me feel you in my arms and against me. Love me. Love me. Oh, Jess, love me, now."

And she did. She put her hands on his head so gently. She kissed him back and held him. He shivered with his desire. Was it for her? Or yet again was it only for release?

Her body wasn't interested in debate. It wanted him with such lust that she was shocked. If her body was that hungry, why was her mind trying to be aloof? Not all of it was aloof. Some of her was avidly aware.

She gasped with the thrill of him. She found her hungry body rubbing against him very like a wanton woman. Her stomach was aware. It felt his hungry sex, and she murmured in her throat in such a way that he groaned as she deliberately curled her hips and pressed against him.

Her fat, interested breasts were squashed against his hard chest and they were very tender, but they wanted the feel of him. And it didn't matter that they hurt because the hurt was changed and turned into lust.

By then, he had his clothes off, and he was trying to get hers off in a subtle manner. It was almost as if he didn't want to make her aware of what he was doing. Now? How could he be so clumsy?

She let go of him and helped. It was a little startling to get naked with a naked man. In the several times in those years that she'd allowed something sexual to happen, she'd always had on *some* sort of discreet clothing. She had never before been stark, staring, completely naked with a man. It was sobering. The idea of it cooled her.

He wasn't cooled.

He got her into the guest-room bed. He put his hot hand on her stomach and swirled it. It felt... marvelous. She asked, "How many stomachs have you rubbed?" She was delaying by being sassy.

But he replied thoughtfully, "I don't remember ever doing that—before now. Do you like it?"

"I love it. Do it some more."

He did, and she purred like a cream-fed cat. Her body moved. And it was very similar to a horizontal belly dance.

He was jittery and breathing heavily and shivering. His hands shook. He had her naked. *And he'd already gotten her into bed!*

He said, "I'm not sure I can wait. I've got to get the condom on. I—"

It was too late to be careful. He didn't need a condom. Not now. She said, "It's okay."

He asked, "Not all safe periods are that safe."

She could vouch for that quite easily. She said the truth. "This is."

He was cautious and it cooled him a little. "Are you sure?"

"Yes."

"I don't want you to get pregnant."

She chose the words. "I won't this time."

He smiled. "Maybe we will another time?"

She asked, "Who knows?" And she shrugged in a very eye-catching manner.

"Ah, Jess, you can't know what this means to me, to have you in my arms and to have you against me this way. You are so wonderful. Are you sure this is okay?"

"No problem."

He sighed a long relief. "I'm so glad." He hugged her close and nuzzled her. She reheated fast, as he allowed his mouth to venture over her and about drove her crazy.

She began to make little, hungry sounds and move against him.

He said, "Pretty soon, now, don't let's rush."

"Let this time be quick and we'll take time the next one."

"Wow!" he gasped. "Don't scare me like that! Are you voracious?"

"Maybe."

And he laughed low in his throat as he gathered her under him. He rubbed against her before he whispered urgently, "Place me."

She rubbed him on her and then placed him. And he sank into her with a gasp. He paused and breathed, holding very still, very carefully.

And under him, she began to wiggle.

He said, "Hold still."

And she said, "Next time."

So it was rather quickly done. They immediately panted to climax and shuddered as they gasped and shivered. Minutely, their muscles loosened as they relaxed, and their harsh breathing slowly, slowly quietened to sighs of repletion.

After some silence, she said, "You weigh a ton."

He stirred and replied, "That's not couth of you to try to make a man in my position laugh."

"You ought to be on the bottom."

"Next time."

"Now?"

He cautioned, "Don't scare me that way."

Her throat chuckle was so amused. She loosened her grasp on him and relaxed in a way that was thrilling to him. She put her hands into his hair and petted him.

He pretended to purr. He didn't know how. He did a lousy job of it. But he didn't move off her. He lay completely spent.

She observed, "You lose interest pretty fast."

That old saw. He said, "Ummm," in savoring. "You're just lucky that I shaved before seeing you."

"I like whiskers."

He stilled. "Whose?"

"My daddy used to whisker us kids."

"Anybody else?"

"Not that I recall."

He said, "I don't believe I can get up off of you. We might have to lie this way for a while, until I can recover...enough. If you remember, I went right to sleep after that first time."

"Out cold," she agreed and her voice was tender.

"How'd you get away?"

She explained, "You pulled off me and lay over to the side."

"How nice I was at least that courteous. What are you planning to do with me now?"

"Wait?"

He laughed so helplessly and moved a little to take some of the weight off her. "You're wonderfully female. Do you realize that?"

"I've known for some time that I was a woman."

He agreed contentedly, "You're made for this. Why aren't you married?"

How was she to reply? "No one I wanted asked."

"What about those who wanted you?"

"I tried one. It just didn't work. He wasn't really husband material."

And he instantly asked that same old male question, "Who was he?"

"No one you know."

"Well, I've only been here twice." He put his face down close beside hers as his voice got husky. "And I was mesmerized by you. Are there other women in this place?''

"All kinds."

"Should I look around?"

She didn't reply, and he moved on her, lifting his head and bracing himself on his elbows. He asked more seriously, "Should I?"

"It would have to be your choice."

He admitted gently, "Actually, for the sake of customs, this is too soon."

"You could look but not touch."

He pressed against her. "Is this called touching?"

"Another word entirely."

"Do you know those words?"

"Some of them."

"I am shocked." He kissed her. "Was I too fast for you?"

"You were trailing a long way behind me."

As a teacher, he was explicit. "I was in front of you."

She laughed an intimate throat chuckle that was very toe-curling. How could she be so man-hungry? Actually, her body was hungry on its own. It was her choice that she wanted only Zach.

Her hands moved on his head in a light, sweetly slow petting. Her face was vulnerable.

He leaned down from his elbow support and kissed her lips softly in sips. His face became quite serious. He groaned, "Ah, Jessie, you are magic."

In that position, she managed to shrug. "I was available."

"Don't downshift me. You know how special you are." His tone had been chiding. Then curiosity crept in, and he asked her with interest, "Do you know?"

"I'm a hungry woman. You are a man."

"How'd you know that?" He pretended to be indignant.

"I've had you before and you fit just right."

"Yeah. I guess I did at that. How did you come into my radius at such a crucial time? It was release I needed—"

"Yes."

He was very serious. "But this time it was *you* that I needed."

"There is a difference."

He smiled and moved his body on hers. He had not diminished at all. He was still tautly inside her. He swirled a bit. "I couldn't possibly do it again this soon." Then he swirled again. He was reluctant to leave her. "I should leave you and let you, uh, catch your breath?"

"Why?"

He laughed. He put back his head, trying to smother his laughter. And he just put his forehead on hers and laughed with a closed mouth. He was sure no one would hear them, laughing that way.

And gradually their encounter became more concentrated, more intense. Their bodies reacted and stirred. Under him, she moved like a human snake.

She loved his hairy chest on her bare breasts. She loved his hairy stomach on hers. She loved his loving. She sighed and moved her hands on his back and head as her shoulders and hips encouraged his attention. The insides of her thighs rubbed his hairy legs.

He became riveted. That surprised him considerably.

Their breaths picked up as their sexual tension increased. It surprised him even more. And they made love a second, slow and exquisite time.

They slept.

He did slide off her and they were side by side, and their sleep was peace. Sated peace.

How amazing that she punched her tiny alarm clock at the last minute. It was habit. She napped when she was exhausted but always limited the day sleep so that she would sleep at night. She'd given them a half hour.

With the slight buzz, Jess wakened. But Zach was out for the count. She tried to waken him, but he was flaccid and unresponsive. If he hadn't been breathing like a male, she could have been concerned.

But the flight down to Sea View, the coming confrontation of fact the next day and the lovemaking with Jess had sundered him altogether. He was out.

Jess considered what she ought to do that would be logical and not keep him scandalously there that whole night. She got up from the bed and tidied herself. She pulled on her discarded clothing so that she wouldn't tempt him again. How could he after *two* such sessions?

One never knows about what a hungry man can do.

The cat yowled again. Again? So that was what wakened her even before the buzz of the timer. The cat had yowled. Her cat never yowled to get inside. She went into the kitchen and saw the blocked cat door.

Um-hmmm.

So he'd been prepared? And she grinned as she shook her head at herself. What was she doing?

Five

———

After Jessica let the indignant cat back inside the house, she ignored the snide comments and went back to the guest bedroom. She stood by the bed and looked down on the sleeping man with possession.

Possession? How could she feel possessive after knowing a man such a short time on only two brief and different sexual occasions? He did not belong to her. She only carried his baby.

Jess put her hand on her still-flat stomach in a comforting way. She sought to soothe the man's baby who grew hidden there, inside her. And it was only then that she felt a tiny wiggle.

Was it the baby? Or was it only a bit of gas? Who could tell? It was in the book the doctor in Corpus had recommended. The book said she wouldn't be able to discern a difference. Not at first.

Was she being comforting to a bit of stomach gas? How droll. But, ah, the father lay deeply sleeping, there on her bed. He lay on the guest-room bed. It was not her own. Not the bed she slept in. How interesting that they hadn't gone to her room.

Actually, the only reason they hadn't was because her bedroom had been farther away from the living room. The guest room had been handier. Jess had to smile at Zach's eagerness. His hunger. His marvelous cooperation. And Jess was admitting that she had intended seducing him. It had been deliberate.

Her mesmerized attentions were interrupted by a really snide yowl from the tomcat. He was starving.

She swept the intruder off Zach's bed and into her clutching hands, and quickly got the cat out of Zach's room. His room? It was the guest room.

Zachary Thomas was her guest.

Jess noted the time as she fed the cat dry cat food. That had replaced the usual canned cat food. The cat was not thrilled. He snubbed the dry food and gave her a narrow-eyed look of disdain.

Cats do that quite well.

She said aloud, "This stuff doesn't stink like the other did. I've put those cans away for now. There could come a time when I might be able to stand the stench?"

That was the TEXAS questioning statement.

The cat did not comment. He snubbed the junk in his bowl and walked stiff-legged back out the cat door.

Obviously, he had already eaten something somewhere else. Jess dumped the dry food back into the box and put the box into the pantry. The mice would have to work harder to find it there.

Jessica did not like mice. At all.

So, freed of domestic duties, she went right back to the guest room. By checking her watch, she found she could look at Zach for about seven and a half minutes before she must waken him.

And she did just that. She stood and just watched him sleep. Jess wondered if any other woman did that. She couldn't recall any of the women she had known who had ever said, "I watched him sleep."

Men are another race entirely. They are so strange. Why would women— Well, she certainly knew why. It was a head-shaking smile that crept onto her face, widening her eyes. She was mesmerized so foolishly by this man. Why him? Why this man, Zachary Thomas?

And she remembered that first night at the hotel, when she'd stood and looked down on him sleeping. And her sated, purring body had loved his body's attentions, even then. What was so magical about Zachary Thomas?

She didn't try to figure it out; she just smiled down on him. Her eyes went over his body and his face. She drank of him, filling herself.

He would leave.

It was a weekend. Not only Zach but the harvest recipients or their parents had obligations during the week. They had come there to thank Zach.

Tomorrow would be a rough day for Zach, who was her love.

How tempted Jessica was to just allow him to stay right where he was, to sleep in the peace that now surrounded him. She could call her friend Mim to come share the role of chaperone.

But Mim was a looker. She was so stimulating to males that she'd probably unknowingly steal Zach's attention away from her. And jealousy sneaked up inside Jess. How average of her to feel such a stupid competitiveness. How useless to think she could keep him.

And Jess began to consider what Zach would think of her if he ever found out that she was pregnant. Or would he ever come back or contact her in order *to* find out? Actually, there was no need.

But he might want to know about a child that was his.

That was something she would have to face. Sooner or later.

Then she just spent the remaining microseconds in absorbing how he looked, there in bed, surfeited from lying with her.

He hadn't just lain with her, he'd been quite busy and very active. Ummmm. Yes.

It was time to waken him.

The next morning, Zach was having breakfast at the hotel when Jessica arrived at The Horizon Hotel. She saw him and was observing him sitting at one of the dining room tables when he looked up and right at her as if he was guided by radar. He put his napkin aside and began to rise from his chair as he smiled at her.

She smiled back at him and lifted her hand, but she shook her head and turned away to her office behind the hotel desk area.

She had no business there. It was Saturday. She had simply been incapable of staying at home and waiting for him to call her. She'd wanted to see him.

He was due to leave the hotel about nine-thirty. The meeting with the harvest recipients would be at the hospital at ten. Zach was to be there a little earlier in order to see the staff doctor first.

As Zach had requested, Paul would be there. So would Jessica.

The TV cameras were also there. Harvesting of organs, bones and skin was sorely needed. Too many people weren't prepared to write the directions in order to be a donor. Who dies? It's always a startling occurrence. Not enough people make plans.

With Paul and Jessica as observers, Zach met with the doctors and harvesters first. They had sent Zach information on their projects. He was primed. The edited meeting would be on TV. It was done to urge people to give their consent to the harvesters, while they were living.

The doctors advised Zach to listen to the children. If he listened, he would understand how important the gifts from Mike had been.

Then Zach met the children and one female adult who were the recipients. Paul and Jessica faded into the background with the discretion of savvy adults. They watched.

The cameras were discreet. The camera people said they were focusing and testing angles. The children and Zach talked. It was emotional for Zach. Each of the recipients told him how they'd been helped.

Each person held a part of Mike.

The gathering was animated and enthusiastic. They had no qualms about showing Zach Mike's contributions... on them ... or where, in them. It was only by concentrating just on the live children that Zach could listen and watch.

But through them, Mike lived.

Zach had been prepared to talk about his wife and son.

But he did not.

As a teacher, he found himself asking the children questions. And the children were comfortable with Zach. They talked and laughed and showed off. They touched Zach. They leaned against him. He asked them questions about their schooling, and they competed in sharing his attention.

It was a noisy, laughing time. But then they thanked him. Zach smiled at them and looked at the *person* whose life had been changed. He would think of Mike—later. Zach was in control of all but his tears, which puddled at the bottoms of his eyes, and, on occasion, one would spill. But he went on, concentrating on who was speaking.

It was a remarkable time.

The only one absent was the recipient of Mike's heart. That one had broken a leg, running for a ball. She'd never run before. They'd warned her to wait until she had practiced and was used to running. But the heart was strong. It had only been a wicked, careless fall. Well, she'd given no thought to running before then.

There was a tape of her. Her name was Eileen. She was a fragile little wisp, in bed with her leg in traction. Her eyes sparkled and she was so amused that she'd broken her leg. She was restless in bed.

Mike had been like that.

Ah, but Mike's heart hadn't changed the child. She'd probably always been restless inside that fragile body. Mike's heart had only helped that restless little girl run! And running, she'd broken her leg.

On the filmed bit, Eileen ended up saying, "I'll see you later." And from the screen, she threw a big kiss with a bony little hand.

It almost unglued Zach. He smiled and licked his lips. He threw a kiss back to the screen, as the little voice yelled, "Thank you!"

Zach took a careful breath and looked back to find Jessica. He looked at her mushy smiling face soberly, gaining strength from seeing her. Then he looked at Paul. From him, Zach got control. Nothing caused Paul to waver. He was staunch.

But when Zach turned back to the children and the one adult recipient, Paul swallowed, breathed and quickly wiped his eyes on his handkerchief and discreetly blew his nose. Paul had known the functioning but unconscious Mike only briefly. Paul's compassion was for Mike's father.

It helped Jessica for Zach to turn back to the recipients who were chattering and laughing. They were used to strangers, and in sharing the gifts from Mike, they felt bonded to each other. It was very nice.

The one young adult female said it all. "We share. We're like brothers and sisters. We're kin because of Mike." And she included Mike's father in their closeness.

They all agreed to that. They laughed and were a little loud. No one hushed them. No one scolded them. Until they became too loud and then Zach quietened them. He began to quiz them on their studies.

The TV people got some great film. And they were so discreet that no one paid them any attention.

The time flew.

The recipients, with Zach, Jess and Paul, had lunch together there at the hospital, and they parted in exuberance. They would meet again, another time. But they had arranged a way to communicate in the meantime.

The children and the one adult all hugged Zach. It was really something special.

Zach was wrung out and yet his spirit was lifted in the most extraordinary way. How strange.

With the recipients gone from the building, Zach shook Paul's hand. "I don't know what I would have done without you standing there like a rock to keep me from coming apart."

Paul shook his head. "You wouldn't have. You were just as excited as the kids to share Mike with them."

And Zach said, "Yes."

Jessica's hand was held by Zach's other hand. He wouldn't let go of her. His right hand was free, and he hugged Paul. "Thank you for coming. I can't say that enough. You've meant so much to me in these last few months."

Paul said soberly, watching Zach, "—and Jessica."

Zach smiled and looked down at her. Softly, he repeated, "And Jessica."

Paul said, "I have to go. Behave."

Zach blinked. Then he smiled. "Yeah. Thanks, Paul."

"I'll be around."

Zach reminded Paul, "I'll be leaving tomorrow morning at eight."

Already turned away, Paul called back over his shoulder, "I'll be at the field."

Zach watched Paul stride off. "He's been such a rock for me."

Jessica commented, "You use that word for him."

Zach looked back at her to add, "And you. Thank you for being here."

She countered, "You didn't need either of us. You were the rock."

"I needed you both. Without you here to watch over me, I'd have bawled like a newborn, orphaned calf."

She scoffed, "Just breathing this air, you're getting TEXAS genes piling up inside you. When have you ever seen a bawling calf?"

And he replied with indignant aloofness, "On TV!" Then he sassed, "Fooled you there, didn't I?"

"Yep."

"You-all taught that kind of talking at birth?"

"Yep."

But Zach changed to saying earnestly, "God, Jess, wasn't it amazing to see those kids and know Mike helped them? How wonderful of them to share it with us."

Jess was touched that he had included her, the hospital staff and the cameras.

But then he said, "It was very important for me that you were here. I'd have probably cried if I hadn't had you here watching me. If I'd cried in front of you, I'd have been embarrassed."

"Pooey. You can handle anything."

"You. I can handle you."

Her hand was still in his and she squeezed his. "You were superb. You made it easy for the kids to be glad."

Thoughtfully, he repeated her last words. " . . . for the *kids* to be glad." He mused on it as he nodded, and then he told her, "That's a good way of putting it. I was really paying attention to them in order to protect myself and not bawl and make an ass of myself."

"You wouldn't have. Mike is still a very living part of the world. Under those helpless circumstances, it was lucky the hospital could help those kids and that lady."

"Is she old enough to be called a lady? She seemed pretty young."

Jess replied, "I think she's nineteen."

So he asked, "How old are you, again?"

With some droll patience, she replied, "Ten years older than she."

Zach nodded, and they walked along to the exit. "That's mature."

"Be quiet."

Zach grinned at her and swung her hand.

They exited the hospital complex and Zach stopped to breathe deeply. "I'm alive again."

"Haven't you been?"

And he looked down at her soberly. "It's been a strange time. Grief? Abandonment. A lost feeling. Or a feeling of being lost. Left behind?" He tugged on her hand and walked along away from the hospital toward the beach in the afternoon TEXAS sunshine.

As they walked, Zach mused on words. He spoke aloud and gestured with his free hand. He was talking not to her but to himself. For himself.

He said, "This has been a—different—time for me. Unreal. As corny as it sounds, it's been a dream time. A nightmare time. I thought I'd waken and everything would be the same as it had been." He turned to Jessica and said to her, "Even the magic of being with you hasn't seemed real. Are you a dream?" He was frowning and serious. Vulnerable.

Quite logically and openly, she replied, "I'm real, alive and very human." She didn't mention she was also pregnant with his child. To tell Zach such a thing at such a time? What would that gain?

Zach was still in a middle world of human grief. He wasn't dead or alive. He was not really in *this* world. He functioned. He worked. He communicated. He suffered.

But he was healing. He could communicate and respond, but living as he was in a strange halfway place must all be very odd to his mind.

Or did he simply function, doing what he knew he could do? Not having to think beyond tomorrow?

It was a good thing she hadn't mentioned the baby now harbored within her body. Having a woman pregnant at this time was not what he needed. Nor did she need him.

He would leave. He would heal. And his life would go on.

So would hers.

And so would the little life she nurtured. Was her understanding of Zach and his circumstances what caused her to keep the baby a secret? Why?

It was too soon for Zach to know. She could handle the baby by herself. What man could lose a wife and child in a fatal wreck only to almost instantly impregnate a stranger? How would that be for a— schoolteacher?

His life could be turned upside down. What would the students think of such conduct? What negative influence? Jess didn't even know whether she wanted to share the child with Zach. She only knew that her body liked his. That was hardly a reason to get involved with a man.

Of course, a child was a good, serious reason.

Well, she'd think about such a problem at another time. Zach wasn't the only one whose life was tilted. Hers had been tilted. By Zach.

But Zach's wife and son were dead, gone. Jessica's problem was a living one.

Zach wasn't yet emotionally ready to hear about such a shock. His basic body had hungered for hers. Actually, it hadn't been for *her* body but for any woman's. It had been simply for a mindless relief. Jess understood that clearly. He'd just wanted surcease. That was only sex. And she admitted that she loved sex . . . with him.

As she and Zach walked along the beach, it came clear to Jess that Paul was aware Zach was taken with her. Paul didn't approve. Paul was a good family man. He volunteered his time to people who needed help.

Jess musingly wondered if Paul's wife minded him going off to help other people and standing by them. His wife had the responsibility of their house and children mostly alone? Hmmm. That was an interesting thought.

And Jess remembered how frantic Paul's wife had been, as all that first day, Paul had stood silently at the hospital as support for Zach.

Yes.

Paul did a great deal in helping others. Which would Paul choose if his wife needed him when some stranger did? As he had with Zach, would Paul choose the stranger? Probably. He had so chosen on the day of Zach's wreck.

What a misguided do-gooder was Paul Butler. There had been all those skilled people at the hospital who were quite capable of taking care of Zach. They were trained to. But Paul had been there instead of at home keeping the kids quiet and helping with the dishes or laundry or whatever.

An interesting observation.

Paul was a public do-gooder. He probably complained to his wife about the way she ironed his shirts . . . while their kids pulled on her jean legs and cried.

Jess watched Zach as they walked down the sand above the lapping waves. He didn't really look at any child. There she was, pregnant with his baby, and he wasn't really interested in those around him.

He took her hand. They walked silently up the beach away from people.

He looked down at his feet as he walked. Where was his mind? He looked at her. "I'm glad you're with me."

"Paul would be if I wasn't."

"I worry about the time he gives me when he has a family. Why would he feel such compassion when he came on to the scene in the dunes? Has he lost anyone to a wreck?"

She shrugged her shoulders. Had Paul? She didn't know. He was older than his wife by ten years. Before they met, maybe he'd been a witness at a similar wreck. It is so easy to judge another but it is hard to be accurate. Assumption isn't always right.

Was she maturing?

Was it the prospect of being thirty years old or was it the fact that she would be responsible for a life other than her own?

They went on up the dune-warped beach. The sands were rearranged by the winds and the tidal waves. The sea-washed beach was sloped and the waves ate at the sand.

The gulls thought the area was theirs. There were pelicans and whooping cranes. There were all sorts of invaders. Or were the humans the invaders?

We think that wherever we go, the land is ours.

Zach said, "Do you feel we are intruding?" He gestured at the various birds. There were even sparrows. What did they find on the sand? How busy they were.

She replied, "I think of the beach as mine."

He nodded. "I can see that. But the birds were here first."

"Not these birds. They aren't as old as I by any count. They are relatively young and pushy. They quarrel with one another and are arrogant."

"Birds? Pretty feathered birds are arrogant?"

"Watch them preen."

He scoffed, "They only do that because it's such a nuisance to tidy themselves. We just hop into a shower and it's done."

"Oh, you stupid male. Have you no idea at all what it takes to look good?"

He chose then to comment, "You're skinnier than you were. Are you okay?"

"Yes."

His voice became husky. "It would rattle me considerably if you are not well."

The queasiness was almost past. She was eating better. She smiled and told him, "I'm just fine."

Zach swung her hand between them and smiled at her. "It has been a treat to see you again. Could you come see me in—say—about five more months? Wouldn't it be okay by then for a man to begin to—look around?"

He rather shocked her. His wife had been dead three months! But in five months, Jess's stomach would be round bellied and obvious. So, she said, "I doubt it."

His face changed to shock and he asked, "Don't you like me?"

"Well, yes. But, you see— Well, it would be awkward."

"So you are involved with another man."

"No."

He watched her from under his eyebrows and he was very serious. "You could come up to visit."

"Not now."

"Well." He didn't add to it but walked along holding her hand more securely as if she might pull it loose and run away. He looked around for a time, sorting words. Then he said, "I'll be back."

She could have easily cried. Crying had been a nuisance for some time but it was over him this time. She breathed carefully and looked around and counted in the multiplication tables to distract herself from the silly old emotional tears.

People think men have it rough. They are generally male when that is discussed, but they don't get pregnant and they don't have to deal with other men!

Actually, they do deal with other men and do it quite easily. It's just women who have trouble with men.

She frowned and slid a censuring glance his way to singe his male hair.

But he wasn't looking and the glance was wasted.

He told her, "I can't get back here very easily. It could be months."

"There's the phone."

"Would you call me?" He looked at her in a vulnerable manner. With a woman, men can do that well, indeed. It isn't even deliberate.

She smiled only a bit and said, "I could."

Zach was very earnest. Very serious. He reminded her, "You have my number. If you call and I'm not there, you could leave a message. I'd call you back."

She smiled. "You needn't feel obligated to me. I've enjoyed our—encounter."

He was emphatic. "We made love."

She walked along. Finally, she said, "It was a little sudden."

He speculated as he looked around the beach, up and back, as men do. He told her, "I think my guardian angel wanted me to notice you while I had the chance."

"Do guardians do that?"

He looked at her, astonished. "Why else are they around?"

She came—that—close to replying that guardians guarded us from harm. How could she say that to Zach when he'd lost his wife and son? So she said, "Ummmm." Which was meaningless.

Zach said, "I think we're far enough away."

So Jessica turned automatically to begin the walk back.

He asked in shock, "Where are you going?"

She looked back at him in some surprise.

He was logical. "I've never done it on a beach. I need to widen my experiences with you."

Ummm. The hotel, her guest room and now the beach? She'd be on the bottom in the sand.

He was watching her with the slightest smile of anticipated carefulness. If she declined, he would walk back with her and find a discreet bed somewhere. Her house? Not the hotel.

And she was thinking, her first time had been on the sand. It wasn't the best of beds. But if she did this with him now, he would remember her for the rest of his life.

Well, he would remember her name for a while; then he would have to search his memory and find her. Then he'd finally only remember he'd done it with a female down on some coast's sandy beach.

At best, memories are unreliable.

She grinned at Zach and said, "On the bare sand? I'd get grungy."

Being a logical man, he suggested, "We could go into the water and freshen up."

She commented with some adultness, "Do you realize that saltwater—"

"Let's live for the day."

How typical of a male who is just about always on top.

Six

***

Zach had obviously had absolutely no hesitancy in, uh, disrobing. He unzipped and shed all that civilized facade. He looked very natural—stark, staring naked.

She did stare. He was magnificent.

He was earnestly more specific. He urged, "Don't be afraid of it. You've been friends several times and it isn't that bad. It's just anxious."

She laughed in bubbles of sound. She blushed. But then she was about that color anyway just being pregnant.

Was the face flush from embarrassment? Was she so self-conscious of being pregnant that it had caused her face to pinken? Or did she flush because she was redheaded?

When she managed enough nerve to face the family doctor, she'd inquire.

Jess looked around and as far as she could see, they were alone. How basic. There were the dunes and there were the grasses with the dune's crawly vines.

So Jess was some surprised as Zach took her clothes and combined them with his, as he made a bed for her. She watched him as he smoothed the sand and lay the materials just so with her soft, U.S.-made silk underwear on top.

The surprise came when he lay on the bed to test it. At least, Jessica thought he meant to test it. Then he held out his hand to her and said, "Now."

Just his movement and word were an aphrodisiac. The thrills stirred inside her own sex. Since he'd gotten her pregnant, she'd been somewhat startled by her sexual hunger. She was ready for him.

On rare occasions, there can be impressive ice and snowstorms in TEXAS. But the great amount of winter wind in TEXAS is gentle and kind. It was so to their naked bodies. She took Zach's hand and went down on her knees by him.

He lied, "Lie on me. I'm softer than your bed."

Sure. The sand would be better than his hard muscle and bone body. She asked, "I get to be on top?"

He gave her a careful, honest look. "I'm softer."

How ridiculous! She scoffed and rolled her eyes in disbelief.

"Try me!" he invited. "I'm like a cloud."

Her chuffing laugh was sexual. She then arranged herself so that she could lean over and lie on top of him. She wasn't practiced and had to adjust herself somewhat.

He noted that. He smiled and helped and put his lower lip under his teeth to keep himself from snorting like a randy goat. He smoothed her onto his body and groaned in what sounded like agony.

She thought she was too heavy and said, "I knew this wouldn't work. Let's try it the—"

"No!"

"But—"

"Hush. Lie down and let me get accustomed to having you on top."

She shivered with need.

He was aghast. "Are you cold?"

She blurted, in all honesty, "I want you."

In a choking gasp, his breath drew in and held as he was wobbled sexually by the very idea that she wanted him so badly. How could that be so amazing? He'd had her. He was almost familiar with her. He knew what she liked.

He asked, "Can you do it on top?"

She grinned in a lip-biting way, trying to screen her naughtiness, but she said, "I don't know."

And he suggested, "Let's find out."

"It could fizzle," she protested.

"You underestimate me."

That made her laugh again. So as she did that, she did straddle him and, of course, she put her hands on his arms and boldly demanded, "Surrender!"

He did try to elevate his male sound of a tiny little voice, but he couldn't make it. However, he gasped, "Help, help!"

A real ham bone.

Being on top—and in control—was a new experience for the neophyte. She did all sorts of things, and his eyes were avid.

His humor spilled from those eyes, and he gasped! He pretended shock and assault. He said, "Not that!"

He said, "No!" He said, "Lower." Men always said that.

She moved around, shifted about and explored him. The winds tousled her red hair, blowing it around gracefully. She was earnest and very, very curious.

He shivered.

She asked instantly, "Are you cold?"

He replied, "No. Hungry."

That was a surprise. "You're hungry after all that food you—"

"Not for food." That old saw.

She considered as she looked at him, and she gradually began to smile.

It was as if she was a virgin, and he wondered about the several times she said she'd "done it" in the last several years. She wasn't at all practiced. For a woman twenty-nine years old, she was very young when it came to sharing sex.

He put his hands under her armpits and lifted her to him. He kissed her in a mind-boggling way. How did he know to kiss like that? Of course. He'd been married to Hannah for some time.

Then he sat her on his sex and suggested, "Help it get where you want it."

She did outrageous things. She put it in her armpit. Then she looked at Zach in all innocence, and she asked, "There?"

But he countered, "Is that where you want it?"

"I'm not sure." So she put it somewhere else. Then she asked, "Is that the place?"

"Almost." He said that on an indrawn, strangling breath.

And she tried another odd place.

By then, he was shivering with desire.

She wasn't a whole lot of help. Not at all. She toyed with him and taunted him and teased him unmercifully.

He grunted and gasped and managed to survive.

But when she wanted to couple with him, he avoided it and turned her over to lie on her and drive her absolutely mad with hot needy desire.

When she begged, he was cocky. A good word. He was. And he teased her until she got serious and tried to push him over. He laughed and allowed her to do as she chose, and she rode him down.

They covered themselves with a portion of their clothes and lay languid and contented.

Her lips were swollen. Her cheeks were still red.

His eyes were lazy and filled with humor. He said, "Go back north with me."

With some annoyed disgust, she told him, "You know that I cannot. It's far too soon. Hannah's friends would be hostile. Your family wouldn't understand. Let's wait out the year, and then we'll see if this is as we think it is."

By the end of a year, the baby would be a reality. She would see what he would think of taking on a wife who already had a baby. She would test him.

That is, if he was still interested, she would then test him. She looked at Zach with her head tilted back a bit and her eyelids narrowed as she judged him.

Would his interest in her dim as the time passed? His wife of over twelve years was barely cooled in her grave, and he was naked on the beach with another woman. In just three months.

She didn't count that first time they'd shared sex. That had only been his brain-stunned emotion instead of sex.

What would he do if he thought some other man had impregnated her? If he contacted her in nine months, she would find out.

She said to Zach, "I think we ought not see each other until the grieving year is past. We can talk on the phone. But I do believe we ought to give your grief time to heal."

He slid a glance to her as he asked, "You don't want to see me again?"

"Suffering takes time. You can't bury grief along with the dead."

He stared at her. "I'm in rejection of their deaths?"

"Quite probably."

"You're just being kind to a grieving man? How many grieving men have you comforted?"

She didn't take offense. Being naked, her shrug was eye-catching. "You're my first, but it wasn't my idea. You . . . surprised me."

He smoothed her hair and tucked her against him. His voice was foggy as he told her, "You gave me surcease."

"I had no choice."

He sighed rather elaborately. "Are you going to drag up my taking you, so suddenly that first time, for all the rest of our lives?"

"If you're around, I probably would—on select occasions."

"One of those." His eyes twinkled as he watched her. Then he said softly, "You'd probably be worth the irritation."

"Do you have a smooth-talking daddy?"

"He would 'harrumph' clearing his throat behind the evening paper when he thought I was beyond the arguing limit. No sixteen-year-old adult ever wants a father to speak up at a time like that. It makes the sixteen-year-old ponder how his father came by that knowledge."

"He was an arguer?"

"Quite possibly."

She chuckled, and they lay on the clothes bed in the sand and watched the clouds. The wind teased their hair and the gulls called to one another. There were pipings of other birds. It was not silent.

But it was peaceful. It was a wonderful day. Of course, just about all days are wonderful in TEXAS. The area gets nasty weather from New Mexico and from Oklahoma and sometimes from Louisiana or even Mexico, but other than those intrusions, it's mostly the perfect weather from TEXAS.

Jessica asked, "How do you like teaching?"

He took some time to change mental gears, but he replied soon enough, "It's an expanding experience."

"Expanding." She tasted just the word.

"The kids nowadays are so smart and so vocal that they can drive a man crazy. They have all the resources and learn! Then they throw odd happenings of the universe into my face and expect me to reply."

"So you scramble with your at-home computer checking facts and figures to keep up and when they ask, you say, 'Good. How did you find that?'"

He nodded.

She considered before she pronounced, "And then the kid talks, and you listen and correct him gently here and there. Or if he's a real snot, you query him."

He nodded. "Or her."

"Females are always kind to the male gender. We know how fragile you all are."

"Hah! Kind? Who was that screeching banshee who scared the very...spit out of me just recently?"

She raised up in shock, lifting her head and looking around. "Someone assaulted you?"

"*You* did!"

"No!!" She curled her hand up between her naked breasts in a very vulnerable manner. In elaborated shock, she gasped out, "I never lose control. I couldn't have. Surely not. My mother told me—"

"What outrageous things did that elegant lady, who is your sweet mother, tell you?"

She nodded with courtesy at his attempt at TEXAS talk. Then she lectured snippily, "Never upset a male—he can't handle it."

Zach laughed. "What else?"

She gestured as she repeated an obvious reply, "If he's grouchy, feed him. Males are very basic."

"And, if they're hot and wanting?"

Quite readily, she instructed, "You give them a cold shower. One cools a man enough."

Zach lay back and laughed. Then he watched her with wicked eyes. He queried, "Out here, what would you do? No showers."

She pointed with her chin. "There's that there ocean, over yonder? That'll substitute pretty good?" The TEXAS questioning statements.

His voice low, he hovered over her and told her, "You're so special." His voice was low and clogged as he questioned, "Why on this earth would you want me away for nine more months?"

"For your own sake." She regarded him very seriously. "You need the time for adjusting to another kind of living. Right now, you are vulnerable, and you're grasping for any change. Any distraction. Even you must admit that you took me for a distraction, for a rejection of death. You aren't ready for any solid attraction. You're still in denial that your life is changed."

Almost immediately, he told her the worst of it. "The house is empty."

"Yes. You might consider having a stereo on a timer so you don't come home to a silent house."

He was thoughtful. Slowly, he asked, "Are you saying that I want you because then someone would be in the house? And you think a stereo would replace Hannah and Mike?"

"No. But you would be foolish to rush into a relationship with any woman who just happened to be around."

"Do you think you qualify as an 'any woman' acquaintance?"

And she looked at Zach as she replied seriously, "I was there when you needed—a contact."

Zach was very serious. "Jessica. Jessica. You consider yourself a contact? A distraction. A useful acquaintance? A substitute?"

She was equally serious. Nodding, she moved one lifted hand in small circles as she responded, "Variations of those words."

He pushed. "You believe it's your body I need, and I have no real clue as to what you really are nor do I care?"

Jessica watched him. Her clear eyes saw him as the man he was. She replied, "Not at this time. I'm someone away from Indy. Someone who is not known there. Someone in whom you can spend yourself. But

I cannot heal you. You must face your loss and let it go. You can't just push your grief aside and pretend it isn't there.''

''You want me to cry and wail and beat my fists on the wall in protest? Do you want to see me grovel and whine? What do you want of me?''

''I want you to accept what has happened to two people you love. I want you to adjust to another life and not just step across the crevasse and not realize how deep it is.''

''You want me to suffer.''

''The selected period for grieving is a good one. It is a public admission that you've had a rotten experience. You need the support of friends. You need to go through this now, or you will suffer worse later.''

''Now how does a secure, small-town woman like you know all that?''

''We lost my older brother, John. He was fourteen. For years I sealed him away until I finally had to face his loss. It was worse then because everyone else was past it. When something remarkable happens, you are better off if you can stop and look at it and understand delayed post-stress syndrome. You should go to funeral homes—''

His interruption was to ask in some surprise, ''And share—funerals?''

''No. Ask for the pamphlets on dealing with death.''

Thoughtfully, he remembered, ''I recall that I was given some of those.''

''Some of the best advice and comfort are those of the rabbis.''

He looked at her seriously. ''How do you know this?''

''When I finally faced my brother's death.''

Zach held Jessica to him and told her, "Out there in the wreck, I thought I was dead, too. How could they be and not I? How could they go off and leave me that way? I'd worked so hard to get established, we finally had time together and they . . . just . . . left."

"Knowing that is a part of healing. They have gone ahead. They'll be there. It just isn't your time, yet."

He asked her, sober-faced, "When is yours?"

"I hope it's a long way off."

In some part of distress, which showed his grief, he asked, "Will you wait for me? Will you be here when this time you're allotted is up? How do I know I haven't only these months with you? What if you die on me, too?"

She soothed him with gentle words. "I'm a very careful person. I really watch—"

"Do you think I was careless?"

And again she soothed. "No. Ike was. You were the victim. Have you forgiven—"

"No! I think he's a stupid bastard!"

Jessica gently shook her head. "Ah. And he was the kindest husband and father, but—"

"He drove like a maniac!"

She agreed, "Yes."

Zach's voice was by then ragged. "And he killed them both!"

"Yes."

"I was still in shock when Paul came. If I hadn't been so numb, I'd have wrung Ike's neck! He was lucky he was already dead."

"No. You'd have helped him."

"After he killed Hannah and Mike? I doubt it seriously."

She reminded Zach, "You were in shock."

"I wouldn't have allowed the medics to help him. I'd have strangled him." And Zach repeated it, "He was just lucky he was already dead."

Kindly, Jessica chided, "His family grieves for him. He was only a very stupid driver. He was a pushover for his family. They loved him very much. He was such fun. Everything was such an adventure. Even casting his line in the surf to fish was an adventure for him."

After a silence, Zach said, "I hadn't thought about Ike's family."

"They were with you at the hospital."

"They were?"

Jess confirmed it. "They sat in the back of the chapel when you were with Hannah."

Zach looked at Jessica. "They were there?"

"Yes. You spoke to them on the way out, when we left to walk along the beach."

Looking off, trying to remember, Zach admitted, "I don't remember seeing them."

"You were in shock."

He looked at Jessica. "I remember you."

"I was an anchor. You may well relinquish me as you heal. You must not feel committed to me."

He was gently positive: "I love you."

"At least you think so now. I've been a touchstone."

He told her, "You're my heart."

"Your heart isn't healed enough to give to me. You need time."

He sighed deeply and complained, "How can you be so sure about all this when I feel completely dedicated to you?"

"You are desperate for distraction so that you don't have to consider what you've lost."

"If you want me to bury my face against your breasts and bawl, I probably could do that. This conversation is—"

"Is...what." It wasn't a question; Jessica was encouraging Zach to continue with his thought.

"Irritating."

"Actually, it's nudging you to face what you have lost."

"Damn you, I *know* what I've lost! I was there! I *saw* it all! Do you want me to have those pictures in my mind forever?"

"Only now. If you don't face this, the pictures will haunt you at another time in your life. Get past it now."

After a long silence, he asked Jess, "Your brother. When did you finally get around to grieving for him?"

"I was younger than he. I didn't want him dead. So I put aside the fact he was. I pretended he would be back another time. He could have been in San Antone or he could have been in Waco or he was away at school. I didn't dwell on where he was. My subconscious just said he'd be back." She turned out empty hands.

"And it didn't work?"

"No."

Zach was quiet for a while. Then he said, "I listen for them to come home."

"I know."

"I'm to leave here tomorrow."

She nodded. "Don't come back for ten months or better, a year. Come back then."

"How will I know you won't be on your fifth husband by then?"

"I won't."

Zach sat and looked out over the Gulf. Then he looked at her. "You'll call me?"

"Yes."

His voice roughened. "But I can't come back until next year?"

"Next spring."

He finally said, "That's almost a whole year from now. Can you go that long without seeing me?"

"I'll call you every week."

"Every...week," he commented in disgust. "That's sparse."

"If you find some woman who attracts you unduly, you won't have to worry about how I'll feel about it."

"How would you feel?"

"I don't know...now."

Zach began slowly in a very serious, careful way, "If you should find some guy that catches your attention, would you..."

She watched, but he didn't continue. So she asked, "Would I...what?"

"Mention it to me?"

She offered, "I'll make a pact with you. If either of us finds someone who interests us, we'll tell the other. Okay?"

"If I said to you that I'd met some woman who was attractive, what would you do?"

Her eyes were on the sand, so the flinch in them wasn't seen by Zach. She said in a calm manner, "I'd say, 'Oh?'"

"What would that mean?"

And with no discipline at all, Jessica snapped, "That I was too far away to scratch out her eyes!"

Zach laughed and hugged Jessica to him. "I shouldn't make love with you again so soon."

"Why not?"

"Are you sure this is okay raw and bare like this? I do have some condoms."

"It's okay, now."

As they lay replete yet again, Zach asked in a nice way, "Are you going to get out of the car this time?"

She jerked her head around and asked, "Why'd you say that?"

"At the airport the last time, you sat in your car. It was all I had to live on for weeks."

"You knew!"

"Yes. I was so—" He moved his hand in little circles.

She didn't help him. She silently urged his words. After that lecture on grief, she urged committing words from him so that she could chide him? Scold him? She wanted to hear them! She wanted to know that he felt this same alignment of souls that she felt.

He was still searching for the right words. "You were so kind to me. It was as if you were my guardian. You blocked out all the shock. All the helplessness. I've always felt I could solve anything. I was proven wrong. You made it seem as if I could be soothed back to reality."

"You have to do that for yourself. That's why you need the time away from here."

"If it's just the place, why don't you come up north and visit me?"

"It's not the place, it's your emotions. You need to heal first."

"Heal? I wasn't hurt. I got through the wreck without a scratch."

And she told him gently, "Not one scratch is apparent."

"You think I don't miss them? I do. But now I have you to think about. Promise on your word that you will call me every week."

"On my word."

He considered her. "How good *is* your word?"

"Clean, logical, trustworthy, true, all those things you can think of."

"Sassy."

"Actually, I'm not at all sassy. I'm solemn, serious, thoughtful, aware and hard-nosed."

So he asked, "Let me see your nose." He scoffed. "It isn't big enough to be hard-nosed. It's pinched and tilts a little so you're probably discerning and critical." He then added in disgust, "You'd probably tell some innocent guy to behave and wait."

"How strange! I haven't noticed any signs at all about you waiting for—"

"I don't remember anything at all." He faked it. "What did I do? Where am I? What year is this?"

And she told him, "There's probably more truth in what you've just said than in anything else you've said so far. Listen to yourself."

"I had one hell of a time with the recipients of the harvest. All those alive kids—" His voice broke and cracked. He breathed deep and steadied himself.

She agreed, "It was a time of emotion. You did your regular job of rigid control."

He asked in a harshly husky voice, "How would it have been for the kids if I'd cried?"

"There are times when you need to show your feelings. Those kids knew full well what you were going through. It would have given them a chance to help you."

"I should have cried?"

"You listened to them. That was the most important. And they saw your tears."

"I didn't cry!" He shook his head. "I disciplined myself."

"You did a remarkable job of it. You were an iron man with yourself. But you gave those kids your attention. They needed it. You were excellent."

He told her in a level way, "It was the control which you have dismissed and discarded."

"You will use that same control, but you will, on occasion, acknowledge how much you hurt. That is what will heal you."

"I've survived three months... alone." He paused and his voice was harsh. "Isn't that an awful word? Alone."

"Ask mothers of triplets."

He grinned. "You always have a retort. Are you generally that way?"

"How else do you think I could have reached twenty-nine without being married?"

He guessed, "You're a razor-tongued harpie?"

"Yep."

He sighed soulfully. "I must say I'm glad you've admitted that. I thought you were a pushov— No, no, not *that* kind. I just thought you'd believe whatever I said."

"Of course. You're a schoolteacher. You would be honest and true."

He readily agreed. "Yes."

"Except for—"

"Don't spoil that compliment. You're really a very difficult woman that—"

"Yes."

"—gets her own way and gets in what she thinks even if it's no use at all and only an opinion."

"Yes."

"Now, now, don't go spoiling the idea that you might be special. You're indicating that you might be argumentative and opinionated."

"Of course."

He grinned at her. "So you admit it."

Unclothed, she shrugged in that fascinating manner. "I've always been unbendingly honest."

"I've noticed that, just today."

Gently, she admonished, "Watch out for yourself. Pay attention." Then she added, "I'll call you each week."

"Yes, ma'am."

"If you lived in a decent place instead of all that distance, up yonder in Yankee country, you'd know to say only, 'Yes'm,' and let it go at that."

And he immediately said, "Yes'm." And he left it at that, but he smiled and his eyes spilled with humor.

Jessica wondered, with telling him to pay attention to himself and to heal before coming back to her, would she lose him?

Seven

Zach had a great, logical argument for staying with Jessica: "You have a guest room! They could think I was in there while you were in your own room as a gentlewoman should be. And that we wouldn't be sleeping together! like some people might think."

"No."

"Well, you could redo your answering machine and say out bold and bare that, uh—"

Jess waited. Then she inquired nicely, "Forget how to reset the answering machine?"

He replied logically, "I was taken with the thought of you being bold and bare. It gave me a mental picture that I couldn't refuse."

"I'll put my clothes back on."

"No!"

"Now, Zach, how will I get back into the town and to my house . . . naked?"

"The visual is fantastic." Then he added philosophically, "It would probably delay my leaving somewhat."

"You'd have me in bed?"

"I'd be explaining to the population—the adults only—as to why you weren't clothed." He gestured. "The town of Sea View could imagine all *sorts* of reasons for you being naked with me."

"Yes. I can understand the premise, but the reasons would be rather limited to one."

"Actually, there would be sufficient reasons to cause conversation."

She snorted.

So he just went on explaining, "Sex, fine arts, lovemaking, voyeurism, swimming—naked in lieu of suits—appreciation of a work of art. That sort of thing, and there's—" Then he was serious. "We need to watch your reputation a shade better."

"Shade?" She gasped in rather elaborate shock. "We're to pull down the shades?"

"You have a very quick and wicked mind."

Jess smiled. "Yes." She glanced down him. Then she added, "But it doesn't show...on me."

He sighed hugely. "You realize I'll spend most of my spare time up in Indy remembering just such a remark from you?" Then his voice changed and deepened. "How will I get over you and forget you if you can speak so outrageously?"

"I'll practice." She finished dressing.

As he dressed, he looked around and at her through slitted eyes and asked, "What *sort* of...practice?"

"I'll surprise you." She finished brushing sand out of her hair.

He took her hand as they began to walk back down the beach. He accused, "Are you luring me?"

"Casually." She smiled and nodded once.

He considered her. "You're only letting me go the length of your line. Then you'll reel me in when you're ready for me?"

"We'll see."

He stopped and jerked his head to look around in some earnest distress.

Jess asked quietly, "What's the matter?"

"I thought I heard a kid . . . crying."

Gently soothing, she told him, "It was a gull."

"Are you sure?"

"There is a resemblance. You learn to listen . . . differently."

He still looked. But then a gull went overhead and made the same sound. He looked carefully around the area but no one else was anywhere they could see.

They went on down the beach.

Gradually, Zach eased.

And Jess thought what a father he was. It was good that he would undertake his mourning. If he didn't face it then, it would hit him harder when it was uncovered, probably when he wasn't ready to cope with it.

The gentle Gulf winds played in their hair and clothes as they strolled lazily back along the beach. With the teasing winds, they didn't look as if they'd been rolling around on their clothes. They went into town, waving back and calling to greeters, but they went on to her place. There, she fed him supper.

The main course was quiche, which had been frozen. It was sprinkled with chives and had olives, sausage and cheeses. She added a fruit salad and large, homemade biscuits.

She had him drink milk. She didn't have any beer. She wouldn't allow coffee, he might not sleep. He drank the milk.

She explained, "The milk is to keep your bones from sagging." She gently raised her eyebrows for any rebuttal.

He was disgusted.

Jess kept their talk light and easy. Not too much talk. Just enough. He was sleepy and easy. He smiled at her.

"You're sunburned," he told her. "Maybe it's windburned. Whisker burned? You look like a woman who's been teased by some man she likes."

"Who?" she asked sassily.

"Me."

She watched him with a soft, gentle smile she didn't realize was there.

And he watched her back. He said, "I'll call in to the principal and tell him I'm caught by the weather."

She gasped, "In TEXAS? No one would ever in this *world* believe you!"

He told her, "You have bad weather here."

She denied it. "The only way planes are delayed in TEXAS is because the weather is bad somewhere *else*!"

"An open mind is always a good indication of reasoning."

She was kind. "I know."

When he left Jess, Zach complained that he would be lost in that big hotel bed all alone. And she ought to realize she was a rotten hostess to push him out of her house that way.

She agreed cheerfully.

"You know you want me in your bed. You're sending me off because you're a slave to your pristine, small-town reputation."

Softly she made just a sound. What he said then had always been true. She now faced being labeled as an easy woman. But her head bobbed in tiny nods that pointedly dismissed such a labeling.

If Zach only knew, he was lucky she wasn't keeping him there at her house. When the scandal broke and the "who" word took over the gossip for that while, Zach *would* be considered . . . briefly.

However, those at the hotel knew she'd gone up to his room with him, that first time. Would they tell? Who would remember? If she could get past that time frame, maybe Zach wouldn't be numbered as the probable sperm contributor.

The next morning, Jessica staggered out of bed on time and stood in the middle of the room until her head wakened and could take charge. She slept too heavily. The Corpus doctor had explained her body's conduct.

She didn't meet Zach for breakfast, but she went to work and, as they'd planned, she noted when he checked out. She went to say goodbye, and canceled the taxi they'd called. She was available to take him to the airport.

How foolish of her.

She couldn't—not.

As she drove him away, he asked, "Why didn't you walk to work this morning?"

She turned her head to glance at him and guessed, "A faux pas?"

"Yeah."

"Uh-oh."

He gently inquired, "Do you ever take your car to the hotel in nice weather?"

"All TEXAS weather is nice."

"In inclement weather?"

She gasped. "We have that—in TEXAS?"

He bore in rather firmly, "I've seen it in weather reports."

"I believe that is only an adjustment so other states and foreign countries will think TEXAS is not entirely perfect, and sometimes the weather is listed, uh, as inclement? Some people are irritated to be told TEXAS is always exactly perfect."

Zach Thomas laughed. He chortled. He was so amused by her.

However, the day *was* perfect. They arrived at the little shuttle airfield, and there were other people there. Several others.

One man said, "Well, hello there, Jess, you shoulda tole me you was coming out thisaway. I coulda saved you the trip."

"I had my car. It was no problem. I was planning on lunch in Corpus with May Bee, you do remember her?"

"I'd heard tell she's expecting again."

Since Jessica hadn't heard any such thing, she only smiled and blushed as she shook her head a tremor. That way the head shake could have meant anything at all.

Jess then said to Zach, "Since you have company here, I'll go on back." She opened her eyes widely so that she didn't look as stricken as she felt. She smiled and said, "Watch the state lines."

Then she left the silent Zach, who stood dead faced, watching after her.

She hadn't introduced Zach to any of the waiting ones. The one who'd spoken said, "Fine woman, that Jess."

Zach nodded. Just enough. He breathed deeply, and another of the men said, "That's doing it right. Breathe this good TEXAS air. You'll need it to survive the flight out of this great state."

So Zach said, "Are all TEXANS that way about the state?"

And they looked at Zach with interested faces and had the gall to ask him, "What way's that?"

They had made him smile. That's what saved him from their curiosity. They could then go through all the old, tired, un-TEXAN jokes they saved for the uninitiated.

The plane came, and those there escorted Zach aboard and made him feel like a homeboy.

But as they flew over the town, he looked down on Sea View and he actually found her house. But it was her car turning into the lot at The Horizon that made his throat tighten.

Then one of the men sitting in front of Zach said over his shoulder, "You was here to meet with the kids that got the harvesting from your boy?"

And Zach said a rather tight "Yes."

Very quietly earnest, the man said, "That was a good thing you did there. The whole town is proud of you. I know the girl that didn't get to be here, if you recall her?" That was the questioning statement. "Her parents and I spoke to you at the hospital. We'll never forget Mike."

Zach's eyes filled but he smiled at the man. "Thank you."

"Ahhh, man, it's us that's got to thank you. How can we ever make it up to you?"

Taking a slow breath first, Zach told him, "By the healing kids being there." His voice vibrated a little.

There were smiles, nods and nose blowings. They'd all been touched.

At the San Antonio airport, his flying companions all shook Zach's hand and they told him, "Come see us. The whole town loves you."

And that invitation sank into Zach's heart and rested there.

Jess called Zach that night. She said sadly, "I was surprised to see those men at the airport."

Zach changed her mood. "You owe me a goodbye kiss."

She retorted sassily, "You'd already had your share!"

"I did not!"

So the time passed for Zach and for Jessica. They talked but it was on the phone. He'd gotten a timer for the stereo and came home to various kinds of music.

He told Jess, "At first I just had what Hannah liked. It made me think of her. Then I added what Mike liked. That wasn't my kind. Now, I hear what I like. It's welcoming. Thank you for mentioning doing that. It beats hell out of coming inside an empty, static house."

"Good."

"You miss me?"

"Oh, so *that's* why I called! I'd forgotten w—"

"Be quiet, woman."

"You're supposed to just say 'hush' or you'll sound just like a Yankee! Uhh, I'd forgotten. You *are* a Yankee."

"There are a lot of us. Get used to it."

"How're your classes?"

"The kids today are so pitched for information that I have to study all along to keep ahead of them."

"How stimulating."

"You're a rotten woman. You're supposed to sympathize and soothe me."

Jess missed him horrifically.

As the days passed, people began to notice the change in Jessica Channing. "You gaining a little weight, honey?"

At first Jess could say, "Not that I know. I'll have to check."

And in the beginning of her fifth month, Jessica stood in front of her mirror, and the time was there. She couldn't fake it much longer. She was conscious of being watched.

On several occasions, her mother asked, "Are you all right in this?"

Those two last words were about as blatant as Cynthia could be.

And Jessica replied, "Staunch." She was telling her mother she was committed.

So they had communicated without actually touching on the indiscretion that was known between them.

How Jess was watched was the most interesting. People are so amazing. It was the women who mentioned to her that her body was changing. The men only discussed her among themselves. But they watched her from a distance and were hearty around her.

Not Paul. Paul asked, "Do you need any help at all? I'm here."

"How kind of you. I can't think of one single thing." She smiled and walked away.

But the next day she went to her mother. Jess began, "There's something you need to know."

And quite calmly, Cynthia replied, "I know."

Jessica looked at her mother and asked, "What is it that you know?"

"You're...with child."

"Yeah." Jess looked away and for some time, nothing was said further. She looked back at her mother. "I'm pregnant."

"By whom?"

Jess replied gently, "An anonymous person."

"You choose not to tell us?"

Jess nodded minutely. "Nothing could ever come of it."

"Ah, my dear. What have you done?"

With a rather clogged voice, Jessica suggested, "I've collided with the universe?"

Her mother had to agree. "Something like that. You have always strolled to a different drummer."

Jess considered the words. "After John..."

And Cynthia added the avoided word, "—died."

"Yes."

"That was the seed which has made you careless of yourself?"

"I only relinquished John several years ago. I had a hard time accepting his death. I couldn't believe in such a thing happening. Why John?"

"I know. It was just a good thing we had the rest of you."

Again, reluctance made Jess silent. Finally she told her mother, "I have to go to our doctor...here."

Cynthia nodded. Then she advised her daughter, "This will be especially difficult for your dad."

"I am sorry."

"Will you give it up?"

"No."

After some silence, her mother guessed softly, "You love the father."

Jess drew a deep, sad breath slowly and replied as she exhaled, "Yes."

"Who is the man?"

"I'll let you know...another time. He should be told if anything happens to me."

Cynthia breathed carefully and looked away as she gathered herself. "You have chosen a very rocky road."

"It isn't one which is uncommon."

"Here, it's uncommon."

And Jess agreed. "It is a stupid thing for a woman to do. In this case, it was not planned nor was the premise...tested."

"You were raped?"

"No."

"You agreed?"

"No."

"You were forced?"

Jess shook her head. "It was...a surprise. For him, too. It was...very nice."

And with some gentleness, her mother told her, "See if the baby finds that's so."

"Sex?"

Cynthia corrected the word. "Being illegitimate. Life is tough enough for each of us without being a child without a father's name. Not having a father's interest or his support to fall back on. You were very careless."

"Yes."

"You're fortunate that you have a father and a sibling brother living who will back you."

Jess asked, "Not you?"

"In this male world, a woman's backing isn't yet as strong. We still need to be careful of ourselves."

"I admit it."

And Cynthia said, "Of all people and of all my children, I would have thought you the most balanced. You have shocked me."

"Then . . . why are you holding me?"

"I'm anguished for my child."

Jess gulped and tears rolled down her cheeks. "And, I, for mine."

They both cried.

Jess's daddy asked her, "What yahoo did this to you?"

She looked at him seriously and replied with a sigh. "No one around here."

"You haven't been anywhere el— That guy who lost his wife and kid? Is he the one?"

"Why him? He only recently came back here."

"Then who was it?" And his voice carried a shotgun as if it was in his hands.

Jess told her daddy gently, "It's my problem."

"I'm your daddy. You have any trouble with any rawhide, you tell me. Do you hear me?"

"Thank you."

Paul asked her, "Was it him?" Then he didn't even wait for a reply but asked, "Does he know?"

"Who? What? Paul, why don't you put your crutch under your wife for a change and worry over her? She's stretched too far."

And Jess walked off and left Paul standing there, watching after her with some satisfaction.

It was not a good summer. Not for Jessica. There were men who thought she would be easy, and she had a tough time. Her dad had warned her, and he told her to let him know who it was if any male did approach her. But she could not involve her dad in such a time. She told her brother Matthew which clods had harried her. He handled those males quite well...with just a calm warning.

And the town women were mostly avid about her as to who *he'd* been. They guessed. One even guessed Zach's name.

Jess could stop them with a glance but it tore her heart. And she was pinker.

Her sister was surprisingly supportive. As busy as she was, she found time to go to lunch with Jess at the hotel or at the Some Place Else, and she included Jess in her circles.

The first time, Jess and her sister were the only two at lunch. The waitress discreetly cleared the other places away. But the two were still at that big table. Then her sister-in-law came in with a rush. "I thought it was twelve-thirty! The kids were eating when I saw the calendar."

And Cousin Windy came, and after her, Cousin Phoebe arrived. Then Joanne showed up. Joanne was probably her best friend since birth.

Oddly timed tears went along with being pregnant, but it was then that Jessica had a hard time. She smiled. She was very touched.

Their preacher was the biggest surprise. He came to Jess's house. She saw him come up her walk, looking around at her summer flowers and checking out the siding on her house to be sure it was okay. He did that automatically when visiting other single women.

Jess didn't want to open the door to the preacher. She wanted to be left alone. But, of course, she opened the door.

He smiled and said, "Ah, Jess, it's good to see you. Are you all right?"

She stepped back as she said a firm "Yes."

He didn't come inside. He just said, "Would you volunteer—"

She began to shake her head.

"—your flowers for the altar on Sunday? I'd not like the word to get around to Mrs. Burk, but you're the best flower grower in town."

"I'll bring the flowers over on Saturday." She watched him.

He smiled and said, "Thank you. See you on Saturday."

People can be so charmingly kind.

The time passed. People began to accept her with less shock. Just about everyone spoke to her, with her.

And she wore maternity clothes.

The only thing that kept her going was the weekly calls to Zach.

He was easy with talk, and she could hear him getting easier. He told about the kids at summer school. When Jess wouldn't let him come down to Sea View for the summer, he had signed up to teach during that time.

Since most of the kids were retaking some class they hadn't understood, Zach was especially challenged to make the learning carefully structured and understandable. He was truly a teacher.

He didn't just teach facts. He taught how the facts fitted into the stream of life. He taught them how to process information, make decisions, reason and find inferences. Why we needed to know history. Why knowing how to speak was communication.

And to expand the kids he had in summer school, Zach volunteered to take some of the students to the art museum. They went to the Sunday concerts also at the art museum there in Indianapolis. And he took them to baseball games. Teachers do that because some kids are never introduced to such.

Then, too, Zach wasn't doing anything on weekends anyway. And it was great for the kids to be expanded.

Fall had begun when Zachary Thomas came back to Sea View. It had been six months since the wreck. He wasn't supposed to be there. Not for another six months. He'd promised.

Jessica was sitting at her desk at The Horizon. She saw him as if magnets pulled her eyes from her computer.

It had happened again. Jess never looked up. She wasn't part of The Horizon greeters. She didn't care one way or the other about guests. She loved her computer and she loved math. Only Zachary Thomas could touch her subconscious and draw her eyes to him. Every time.

And there was Zachary Thomas coming in the front door with a vibrant stride. There he was! She did not want to stand up and have...him...see her...stomach.

She sat there. She was absolutely furious with him. How dared he come to Sea View in surprise? When he wasn't supposed to come there. When she'd told him not to come for another six months! How dared he!

Even with her neck's resistance, she turned her head away from the sight of him and toward her computer. Her eyes saw nothing. Her hands did nothing. She sat there thinking, *He'll see me!*

It seemed an eon but he came striding to her side. He sat on her visitor's chair next to her desk. She turned her head and stared at him. He was where he should never be!

He was full of himself. He tried not to grin so his face was sassy and his eyes sparkled. He was vigorous and alive!

She hated him. How dared he! Men! They are the cause of all problems ever done!

He said, "Surprised you, didn't I."

She was still drawing in a slow, indignant breath, when he said, "Glad to see me?"

And she replied, "What on earth are you doing here?"

"I got the weekend. I've done everything your way. I've read all the grieving books I collected. And they were all excellent help. Thank you for mentioning them. I had some of them already, but I hadn't read them. It was too hard, then.

"I've thought about Hannah and Mike. I've told them, so long, instead of goodbye. I'll never forget them. I've relinquished Hannah and Mike...enough.

I can think of them without reseeing their deaths. I can remember the good times.

"You were right about everything. I've come to tell you that. You've saved me from some terrible times of loneliness. And thank you again for the idea of the timer on the stereo."

Then he asked with placid confidence, "Can you get the day off?"

"No."

That one word was a clue. He looked at her again. "Is something wrong?"

Her betraying stomach still hidden by her desk, she warned him, "I told you very clearly not to come back until next spring."

That surprised Zach. His eyes became serious and his lips parted just a bit in shock. He just stared at her face.

She blushed. Well, for her, that was certainly no surprise.

With her then silent, he asked carefully, "Can you take the day off?"

And she said, "No."

He was again silent in shock. What had happened? Then he tried to be casual. "I'll go sit on the porch steps with the cat and wait fo—"

"No."

"What's wrong?"

She was emphatic. "You are not supposed to be here at this time."

As vulnerable as any man can be, he asked, "Aren't you glad to see me?"

She was scarlet faced and very serious. "I'll see you in six months."

"What's wrong with now?"

"I told you to stay away until after the first of the year. Go home."

"Jess, what's wrong?"

"You are!"

She was unbending. He stared at her red face and knew he'd really surprised her but not nicely. She was furious with him. Why?

He asked carefully, "Will you share supper with me?" And he hastily added, "Here? At the hotel."

She said, "No. Go back north."

He turned his head away so that he could think. What the hell had happened?

Finally, he said, "I'll go check in, and we'll talk later."

She did not reply.

He rose and hesitated, waiting, but she wouldn't even *look* at him! He slowly moved away, out the office door. Just past the door he turned quickly back and watched.

Jess bent to her lower drawer, opened it, took out her purse and rose from her chair as she kicked the drawer closed in an unkind way. Then she turned and walked away.

Zach saw that she was pregnant.

Eight

Zach was stunned. How could Jess get in that condition without him knowing about it? *Who was the bastard who'd done that to Jessica?*

Zach went out to the car he'd rented in Corpus. He'd driven to Sea View with the plot to take Jess away from her limited town and just be with him.

Who was the bastard who *had* been with Jessica? Was he with her still?

Zach drove carefully, his eyes following her walking figure. But she glanced back. He turned away so that she wouldn't guess he was in a car and following her. He had to find out about her. She was going home.

And he saw Paul. Paul would know. He knew everything that went on in Sea View. He knew more about the residents there than he knew about his own wife, but he was the man who would know about Jessica.

Zach stopped and called to him.

Paul paused and looked at the car. Then he came to it and bent to look at the man. "Zach?"

"Yeah. Where're you going? Get in. I'll take you there, and we can talk."

Paul got into the passenger side, closed the door and settled himself. He looked at Zach's grim mouth and guessed that Zach had seen Jessica. Paul asked, "What're you doing here?"

Zach didn't reply but asked his own question quite savagely. "What bastard got Jess caught?" He used the TEXAS word for pregnant.

"You noticed?"

Zach turned his head slowly and looked at Paul in a very severe manner. And he warned the Rock who was his friend, "Watch what you say."

"If you were TEXAN, you'd say, 'Watch your mouth.'"

Deadly serious, Zach demanded, "Who is he?"

"We none of us knows. She doesn't say. We got tired asking. Her parents are calm, all the guys understand but, well, maybe not the preacher. Even some of the women understand but a lot are—jealous! Fooled you, there, didn't I."

"Who's she going around with?"

"Nobody. You. But you weren't here long enough ago to qualify." Then Paul asked, "You fooling around with her? Is that why you're so hostile?"

Through his teeth, Zach demanded, "Who could leave a lady to face that by herself?"

"That's a good question. You find out and the rest of us'll tar and feather him."

"The damned bastard!"

"The majority tend to agree. He is. But she won't tell. See if you can find out."

Zach let Paul out at his office and drove to Jessica's house. Since she didn't lock her doors, he just walked inside, calling, "Jess? Where are you?"

Silently, she appeared in the dining room. She stood patiently and very unwelcomingly still. She just looked at him. She was furious.

Well, while "furious" wasn't "loving," it *was* emotion. Why was she so angry?

He asked quite gently, "What have I ever done that was so awful?"

Without hesitation, she told him, "You came to Sea View without my permission."

He didn't retort that it was a free country or that he was older than she; however, he did not grovel. "Begin as you intend to go on." He'd been brought up on that excellent advice.

While his mother had instructed him closely in women's rights, he *knew* that he was equal to any female, just as he was to any male. He said, "You are being rude to me. Why?"

An excellent glove-to-the-ground statement.

But what could Jessica say to him? Remind him that on the evening of the day his wife and son had died, he'd taken her and given his sperm to her? He would remember that he had. If he knew the child was the result, how would it be for him? He would feel quite obligated. She said nothing.

He watched as her blush deepened.

"Why are you silent? What have I done to irritate you this much? Why didn't you tell me about the baby? Who is the man?"

She looked at him. She said, "Please, leave."

Zach felt on the edge. He was unsure. How could he declare himself her knight in shining armor when any word might set her off?

"Jess? Am I such an enemy? We are good friends. I care about you. Tell me who is the man? How can I help you? Talk to me."

Her blushing face angry, she retorted, "I told you very clearly that you were *not* to come back here until next spring! I told you that. Why are you here?"

And he was really careful. Instead of stating why— exactly—he said, "I was in the neighborhood?" He had deliberately used the TEXAS questioning statement. But he didn't smile, nor did his voice lighten, and his body stayed rigid in concentration.

Angrily, she repeated, "I told you to come back next spring."

He chided gently, "Why were you hiding the baby from me? Don't we know each other well enough? Am I such a casual friend that you can't share this with me? Are you all right? Do you need anything? How can I help you?"

Great, adamantly forbidden tears began to fill her green eyes.

He groaned, "Aw, Jess, let me hold you." He went to her very carefully, in the way one approaches a rabid dog. He gently put his hands on her shoulders and slowly, carefully pulled her against him. She shivered and gulped, and that made tears come to his eyes. "Ah, Jess."

So she clung to him and bawled out loud without being able to restrain the tears.

He soothed and patted and made throat sounds. He picked her up and carried her into the living room and sat on the sofa. He rearranged her so that she could be comfortable.

He told her that pregnant ladies bawl on occasion. Hannah had done that, too. Life just gets to them. That and hormones. And he asked, "When are you due?"

She gulped and managed, "In December."

"Do...you...see...him?" How very reluctant were those carefully spaced words.

She replied, "Hardly ever." Which was true.

"Then there are no plans...to be married?"

"No."

Choosing his words with hesitant care, he asked, "Was...it like it was at first...with us? Just an encounter?"

"Very similar." That was obviously true.

"Is...he someone...you...love?"

"A stranger." At that time, he had, indeed, been a stranger.

"Did he...like you?"

She continued to be honest about it. "Not really."

Slowly, he confirmed it all. "So you were already caught when I came back to see you. And you knew. That's why you sent me away?"

"Yes."

And his tempo of confidence picked up with the pace of his questioning. "That's why you said I couldn't come back until next spring because that would be after the baby was here? Then you'd present me with the problem, and I could take the package or leave it?"

She took a wavering, steadying breath and said, "Yes."

"Are...you...in touch...with the man?" The last three words were run together.

"He knows about the baby."

"Will . . . you . . . marry him?"

"He hasn't asked me."

And Zach relaxed. He hugged her. He said, "Good. Then marry me."

Jessica was exasperated. Zach had no idea about being a couth adult. It had only been six months since his wife and son had died.

In all good manners, how could he marry her now with her being six months pregnant? There was no way. So instead of instructing him, she told him, "After the baby is here, you can visit and see if you want to take us on."

He was quiet as he carefully went over her words. In shock he stated in slow, amazed words, "You love me." He grinned and said it again, "You *love* me!"

"Hush!"

"*Hah!* I've gotcha! You love me! And you were trying to give me all the outs you could think of so that I wouldn't get trapped into a marriage with a pregnant woman."

As with everything else, she was completely honest. "It was too soon after you'd lost Hannah and Mike."

"Without you, I would have died of loneliness. I wouldn't have had anything to think about." He grinned at her. "So you love me!"

"Don't get carried away."

"Let's get married now."

"It's far too soon. Don't you care about who the father is of this baby?"

"I'll love it." He squinted his eyes and twisted his mouth. "I can probably...well, *maybe* I can share the kid with his father. I'm very possessive. I'll probably be competitive with the other man."

"I love you."

He grinned very big and his eyes puddled. "You scared the hell out of me."

"I didn't want you to know."

He chided her, "Is that any way to handle anything? It was a great test of my character. You really underestimated me, didn't you." It was not a question, it was a goad for her to confess.

"Yes."

"Have...you discussed a...name with the father?"

"You'll be the father, you get to name the baby."

"Good."

So having given him control over the names, she then said, "If it's a girl, let's call her Hannah."

"You're a little too precious. I was thinking more of calling her Cynthia."

Jessica gasped, "You're already thinking of names? I only just told you that you could!"

"If you hadn't, I'd have arm-wrestled. I like naming kids."

"Good heavens! What have I done?"

And he committed a faux pas. He said to the pregnant woman, "Well, you *are* friendly, I can vouch for th— Hey! What's the matter?"

"Don't you *ever* say that to me!"

She was simply furious! And he laughed. How stupid can a man be? He was.

But she could not physically get him out of the house. He was simply too solid. She was so furious that he worried she might hurt herself. So he was calm. How irritating!

She commanded he leave, so he went into the kitchen, took the cat off the table and looked in the refrigerator. He lifted his eyebrows and tasted several things while she went on lambasting him.

Then he turned and smiled at her and said, "You love me. You admitted it. Don't be so angry. You could upset the baby. What's for lunch? Do you like peanut butter?"

"Go away."

"Uh-oh." He sighed with forbearance. "We have adjustments already." He took a deep breath. "We must always have peanut butter in the house." Then he looked at her with lifted eyebrows as if it was her turn next.

How can a woman be angry at such a man? She watched him. He winked at her and went back to examining what was available in the refrigerator. There were leftovers. He sampled. She watched.

He commented with a series of nods, "You're a good cook. That is a solid plus in your favor."

And she asked in a deadly voice, "What are the minuses?"

He tilted his head back as he considered her over his cheekbones. Then he had the unmitigated gall to tell her, "I'll keep track."

He pulled out her chair and seated her at the kitchen table. Then he expounded on his students' brilliance, their challenge, his stimulation—

He hastened to explain, "That stimulation isn't sexual, you understand, that's mental. They're good kids. In this time when teaching is so tightrope-walkingly hazardous, I got a bunch of remarkable kids. We'll see who wins by Christmas."

"Who...wins?"

He nodded as he spread honey on a bun. Then he pulled the honey-dripping bun apart and fed it to her. He explained, "—as to who'll be running the period. They or I."

She watched him. "It'll be you."

He smiled, then he looked over at her. "I needed the backup. Thank you."

"You don't need backup. Whatever it is, you can handle it yourself."

He looked at her. "How can you know?"

"You did it today, with me. Any other man would have had the decency to have left—both times."

"Well, Buttercup, I do love you. And I do know you. I wasn't taking any risks. But I do admit, you sure did make me careful."

She made a disbelieving sound of rejection.

He chided in explaining what she hadn't realized, "I didn't kiss you right away. You have yet to endure that." He smiled at her. "I'm allowing you to be astonished by my control. I've missed you like bloody hell these last three months. How could you stand not to see me?"

She looked at him with pregnancy-induced tears filling her emotional green eyes.

He asked gently, "Or do you mean it when you ask me to leave you alone?"

She shook her head. "I didn't want you to see me this way. I didn't want you to wonder or to speculate or to question me."

"Will you tell me someday?"

"Perhaps."

He watched her. Then he sighed slowly and commented with a hand turned out, "I suppose 'Perhaps' is better than an out-and-out 'No!'"

"You're like Velcro."

He considered and inquired, "Hardy? Reliable?"

"You stick."

Zach laughed but he sobered as he commented, "When I first came here, you told me you were all right. But when I was here in June, you knew you were pregnant. So I couldn't get you that way then."

She chose her words. "Do you accept that I am pregnant?"

He studied her face to judge her question. "I suppose you mean am I jealous or will I ask you to give up the baby or something like that?"

He stared out the kitchen window as he got in touch with his feelings on the matter. Then he agreed, "I am jealous, but the baby is yours and I'll love it."

He regarded her candidly. "That's actual fact. I'm not taking on the baby because I want you. I'd snatch you up if you had a dozen kids." He confirmed that with a serious look into her tear-puddled, green eyes.

He told her, "I'll see him as yours." Then he admitted, "I'll have trouble sharing possession of the baby with another man."

"You do tend to be quite basic."

He smiled. Then he grinned. And he said, "Want to soothe my ego?"

"So *that's* what it's called!"

He chided, "You snubbed me."

"How could you burst in on me without one word of warning? I *told* you not to come here until after the New Year! How can anyone be so dumb as to not follow such explicit directions?"

"You'd make a good teacher in middle school." In an explanation, he elaborated, "It's in middle school when kids begin to believe they can have control of their lives. It's a tough time. We need tough teachers then, if the parents aren't paying attention."

"I remember middle school."

He was droll. "It wasn't that long ago."

"The boys were aggressive. They hadn't learned yet to be subtle."

Zach nodded in a smug manner. "Like me."

She remembered their first time together. There had been no questioning or preliminaries or anything! "I haven't found you that subtle."

He was actually shocked because only his pupils widened. "Do you mean to imply that I was bold and brassy?"

"Yes."

He frowned in self-irritation. "I guess being married to Hannah so long had me on a different track. I'd forgotten a lady needed some courting. Was I rude?"

"No. I wanted you."

He grinned. "Me, too. That is, I really wanted you. I do now. We could, you know. It wouldn't hurt the baby. I'd be careful. You're not having any trouble with carrying the baby, are you?"

"Obviously, I'm not." She'd gone scarlet again.

Zach considered her. "You look healthy. You walk with a good stride. I suppose you're eating like a horse?"

"Since your mother was unsuccessful with you, Hannah should have worked harder on your manners."

"She did try," he agreed. "But the kids in class talk so basic. I have to watch them every minute. However, I do pick up on their manner of speaking! They aren't only basic but explicit! It's just a good thing I'm male."

"What about the girls in your classes?"

"We're talking about the girls! The guys already know not to say those things in class. They've spent time on the hard benches in the principal's reception room. Do you know that one of those boys actually got up a petition to pad those benches?" His face was serious but his eyes sparkled. "I can just imagine how he'll turn out."

"In jail?"

"In politics."

She laughed. Her own eyes sparkled. She was so pink and pretty.

He said, "Now tell me you're glad to see me."

"If I do, you'll be back here every chance, and Sea View will start speculating about—us."

He shrugged and turned one hand openly. "They'll have to start sometime. I'm going to marry you. It would be nice if you are willing and cooperative. No, no, in getting *married!* I've never met such a jumpy woman! Settle down now. Be calm. Honey, you are too sensitive. Is someone being nasty to you? Who? Tell me what's wrong?"

She looked at him with a red face and enormous, troubled eyes.

And his voice roughened. "Marry me, now. I want to be married to you. I love you."

"It wouldn't be proper. Especially for a school-teacher."

"If people think I'm the father, I wouldn't mind. I *will* be the father. And he'll belong to us both."

There was the slightest pause before Zach went on, "I am looking forward to meeting the man who did this to you. No, no. I wouldn't be physical. I can't chide him. He hasn't claimed you. If he had, I wouldn't have a chance with you. I want you to be my wife.''

"I love you, Zach.''

"Come and sit on my lap. I can't stand being clear over here and having you so far away from me.'' By then she was on his lap and his voice changed. "I've missed you. I need badly to hold you and feel you against me. Are you fragile anywhere? How about these? Can I touch them? Let me put my hand on your stomach and feel him move. Mike did that.''

She cautioned, "This may not be a boy.''

"Then she'll quite possibly be a girl! A little girl. After just knowing Mike... You would have loved Mike. Actually, you'd have loved Hannah. Don't ever be jealous of them.''

Jessica admitted, "I tried but it didn't work.''

"You tried not to be jealous?''

She was serious. "I tried to discard them. To push them aside.''

He sorted words. "Don't let them...haunt you. They are...were so curious about everything that they have already said goodbye to me and taken off. They stayed with me through the funeral and went with me back to Indiana. But they left soon after that. If it hadn't been for you, I'd still be alone.''

"So—''

"If you say that I latched onto you because I was lonely, I'll give you a list of women bringing me casseroles who've been hounding me to pay attention to them!''

"Wow.''

Zach shook his head. "It isn't me, it's any man. And they probably figured Hannah had broken me in enough, so they wouldn't have as much work to do on me."

"You feel you are qualified to be a good husband and father?"

"Yes."

She had to laugh, he was so confident.

He smiled back at her. Then he said, "Kiss me. Kiss me and make me know you love me."

So he turned her toward him a little, there on the chair by the kitchen table, and he pressed her to him.

The kiss was as it should have been. Intense. Sexual. Mind-bending. Her stomach kicked him.

That did distract them from the kiss. He leaned away and looked down to say to her stomach, "Don't be rude. I was giving my best shot just then, and you were not supposed to interrupt. I'll deal with you later."

"How?"

He replied logically, "I'll explain individual privacy." He moved his hand out and expanded on it. "Couple privacy, neighbor privacy, intrusive conduct." He frowned down at her stomach and said, "Quit that, kid." Then he looked into Jess's amused green eyes and inquired with some intensity, "Is there one or two?"

"The doctor says only one."

He was incredulous. "And you're thinking 'girl' with a punch like that?"

She shrugged her slender shoulders and her heavy breasts moved. He forgot why he was protesting. He was gentle and sweet. He was skilled and clever. And they moved into the guest room on the bed there.

Her body accepted his intrusion gladly, hungrily, as Jessica groaned. That stopped him cold, but she put her hands low on his back and greedily used him.

It was just fortunate he was so tightly triggered, or she would have left him hyper and riding the glory trail alone. That is, he would lose the chance of sharing the hyperspace fall of expiring lust and have to experience the magic all alone.

Nothing wrong with that.

As they lay in their relaxed sweat on a shambled sheet and summer quilt mess, he touched her carefully and moved his hands gently. He made sounds of pleasure, and her sighs filled his soul.

Since Paul thought they should know, he told Cynthia and Mark to call Jessica and invite her and her guest to lunch. It was a diluting-of-local-gossip move.

Her brother Matthew and sister-in-law Trudy, and her sister Alice and brother-in-law Phil were there. They all pretended not to watch critically in their study of Zachary Thomas.

At first, there were gaps in the conversation, which Cynthia filled perfectly with questions as does any skilled hostess.

But Jess knew that Zach was unduly sparkling-eyed amused.

He loved it. How could she marry a man who understood the human race so exactly?

His selections of comments were remarkable. He soon had them all arguing, not with him, but around the table with intense contradictions. He'd put in a guiding oar, and he knew when to soften exchanges.

He was a teacher. He was practiced. He was skilled. She looked at him. Skilled. Yes. Ah. What a man.

And he was honorable. Did he suspect he was the baby's father? Why would he want to marry a pregnant woman? He was such a puzzle.

Gradually, Jessica became aware that Zach had managed to lure her father into the conversation. He was a newspaperman and a listener. But Zachary had him talking, telling, explaining.

The family was listening to the mostly silent husband, father and father-in-law in some surprised exclaimed astonishment.

Zach had done that. And Jessica watched the man who held her heart.

It was the middle of the afternoon before they even began to clear the table.

Cynthia said to her daughter Jessica, "I have never been able to get your father to talk. Everyone talks to him, tells him things or slips up with some jewel of gossip. He gets to print about a third of what he hears. But I could *never* get him to talk! Zach is a genius."

And Jess replied, "He's a schoolteacher. He's spent some time making kids talk. He knows the buttons to push."

Cynthia smiled and slid her eyes over to her child. "He is something."

And Jess replied immediately, "Yes."

And with her daughter distracted by the man, Cynthia asked softly, "Is he the father?"

"Yes."

"He *is?*"

And the sly woman who was her father's daughter turned honest eyes to her mother and said logically, "Mike was his son."

And her mother's eyes searched her daughter's placid ones and the mother said, "Oh." She said, "Yes," as she turned away.

As they got into Zach's rental car to go to her place, Jessica told him, "Mother asked if you are the father."

Zach hesitated and glanced at Jessica briefly with a careful look that took almost no time at all, but he seemed to slide into the car with hardly a pause. "What did you say?" It was an everyday casual comment to allow the conversation to go forward.

"That, yes—"

Zach's breath intake was startled.

"—you're Mike's father."

"Oh."

And Jessica's father invited Zach to spend the night with them instead of going to the hotel.

Zach said he was already registered. But her father smiled and wasn't at all fooled.

The lovers drove in silence the few blocks to Jess's house. As he parked at the uncurbed side of the street, he suggested, "Let's walk along the beach? Are you okay for that?"

She readily replied, "Of course. I'll change my shoes."

"Me, too."

She turned back and looked at Zach. "I thought you left your things at the hotel."

"I've kept a few things in the car." He smiled at her.

"Like . . . what?"

"My Reeboks."

"Good. I'll get my shoes." She stopped and looked at him. "Everybody in town will be watching us. We won't have any privacy at all."

He laughed. "Is that all you think about?"

She went scarlet again.

He chided, "Don't be embarrassed. I think the same way. And the town is just curious. It's okay."

"It's embarrassing."

"No. It's living."

She considered for a serious minute, then she nodded. "It's true. Curiosity is all that makes the world go around. It's just that *this* curiosity is uncomfortable."

He gasped, "What all do you plot to do to my innocent body!"

She shook her head and sighed elaborately.

But he just laughed low in his throat like men can do in a way that is so alluring to women.

Nine

In TEXAS, it was another beautiful day. Like any good TEXAN, Jessica mentioned, in a kindly superior but sassy manner, "How boring to have such perfect TEXAS weather day after day after day." And she sighed forbearingly.

And Zach had the unmitigated gall to observe, "As I recall, once we walked along this same beach. That was this year! You wore a raincoat, and I carried an umbrella."

She dismissed his words. "You were probably still in grief and walking in Indiana. I understand they have swamps in Indiana?"

He told her gently, "It's public knowledge that there are alligators in the water holes of Texas."

"How you do go on!"

Looking around as men do, Zach then added, "Smart people don't swim in TEXAS water holes.

Besides the alligators, there's quicksand. Do you TEX-ANS actually put discarded people in the quick-sand?''

Jess advised sweetly, "Behave and you'll never know for sure." Then she added with an obvious con-cerned kindness, "TEXAS is always written and said in caps?" The TEXAS do-you-understand statement.

He said a nothing "Oh."

It was spoken like a Yankee who had no cause to be impressed with anyplace or with anything in TEXAS. He lived up north, in Indiana, and didn't need the di-rection on peripheral manners and mores. Since he didn't actually mention such opinions, he was couth enough to pass.

They walked along the beach for a time, seemingly in peace. Then Zach asked with gentle hesitancy, "So... the guy... knows you're pregnant."

And she replied, "He's seen me."

Zach tried to think of how close the bastard had come to Jess to "see" her. Zach must have taken a dozen silent steps along the sand before he asked, "What all does he say about it?"

"He's hesitant and uncertain."

It took Zach a while to actually ask the nagging question. Finally, he steeled himself and asked it in a negative, denying way, "He hasn't offered mar-riage."

"I don't believe he thinks of the baby as his." She was completely honest.

In something very similar to shock, Zack ex-claimed to question, "You sleep around?"

"No."

"You have been with me." His throat sound was the gentle roughness that melts a woman.

"You're a superior lover." She was so sweet.

It shocked him for her to be able to judge conduct. He demanded with some indignation, "How many men do you . . . service!"

But she replied very kindly, "I'm not very experienced." Then she looked at him as she told him, "You are very skilled."

"How many others have you had?"

"Two."

That surprised him. He questioned, "You're twenty-nine and have only had two?"

"Three, counting you. I wasn't interested in any other man for some time—until—you."

Zach asked slowly, "If you weren't interested, did he force you?"

"Uhhh." She concentrated on how to tell him how he'd taken her that night his wife had been killed. "I believe 'surprised me' would be more accurate."

"I can't stand any man who would take a woman without her consent. He must be a Neanderthal."

"No. He's very sweet."

There was some silence. They continued down the beach. Then he asked carefully, "Would you marry him?"

"I doubt it quite seriously. He hasn't shown any real committed interest."

His words came in such an urgent rush, "Then marry me!"

"We'll discuss it next spring."

But he was impatient. "I can't see you having a baby all by yourself!"

She moved her hand in a circle as she listed the mob around her, "My parents, my sister, my brother and his wife, my cousins—"

He interrupted rather hotly as he corrected her words. "I don't mean friends and relatives. I mean having to do all this without a man beside you. Of all times, the man should be here with you, now."

"Perhaps it isn't possible."

He drilled in. "Is he married?"

"He was."

"If he isn't married now, then he ought to do his duty by you." Zach hesitated for some time in an agitated manner that was very subtle. If she hadn't studied him so specifically, Jess wouldn't have noted how upset Zach was. His voice was steely. "Would you marry him?"

"I don't believe he loves me—enough."

Zach changed his words with more intensity and again he told her, "Then marry me!"

She took his hand and smiled up at him. "In the spring."

"You don't want anybody to think I'm the bastard who got you this way."

She lifted his hand to her lips and kissed his knuckles.

He watched her do that with some intense emotion. "Ah, Jessica, how could you let some lout assault you and leave you?"

"He wasn't in control of himself at the time."

"Any real man can control himself all of the time. Men do. Do you think they're never triggered by some special woman? Men have it very tough. But real men know obligation. Whoever the bastard is, who did this to you, he owes you his protection. He— I can't say it. I don't want him married to you. If he could leave you like this and not offer his name, I have no use for him at all. Marry me."

"How can I be sure you aren't just a tenderhearted man who only cares about my circumstances, but who doesn't actually care about me?"

With great, open-faced honesty, he declared quietly, "On my honor."

Very kindly, she took his hand in both of hers as she replied, "We'll see if you still feel the same way next spring."

But he wasn't lured away from the subject. He challenged her. "You'd let the baby be born without a father? How can you do that to a helpless little kid?"

Jess hesitated in telling him the truth. She watched out over the Gulf and she lifted her face to the breeze coming onshore. Finally she told him, "How can I know that you're not just lonely? You may now be willing to take on a pregnant woman, but what about later? How can I know if you want me to leave TEXAS and go up to Indiana and face all of your friends there? What would your parents think of me? Of the baby?"

Positively, certain, he told her, "They'll love you."

"How do you know that?"

"I've told them about you." And he added with a grin at her, "They are very curious."

So she queried, "How can you alter 'appalled' into being 'curious'?"

He chided, "You underestimate them."

"You are only six months from being a widower. How can you know all this so soon?" She was emphatic and spaced the words. "I don't need to be rescued. I need a good man who truly loves me and the baby."

"I love you."

"Your emotions are too vulnerable. Wait. Wait for spring. If you're still of this opinion and you're still free, we'll speak of this again, then."

He became a bit irritated. "So you think this attraction is simply loneliness or rebound or whatever it's called! You don't accept that I'm in love with you, even though I've been back twice now."

He went on, "I came the first time to see if you were real. You are. And this time, it was to see if you could love me. Then I had to be sure you're not getting involved with the father of the baby. You aren't. I have the chance, now, to get you to marry me. If you insist I wait until spring...I could lose you to another man."

He stopped and his anguished eyes met hers. Hers teared and she said, "Oh, Zach."

He told her, "I really love you. It's the forever kind of love."

"It's too soon for you to declare yourself. Wait for spring."

He turned away very disheartened. He took several deep breaths slowly in order to calm himself. Then he looked at her with somber eyes. "You're going to marry that bastard."

She watched him with great compassion. Irritatingly her eyes teared again. Her breaths were unsteady. "I could love you so much that I could die for you."

He instantly gave the solution, "Marry me and save us all."

"Next spring."

And in some impatient anger, he retorted, "Why the hell wait until next spring? You got some fetish about orange blossoms? We can get some from South

America! For the baby's sake, we ought to get married before the birth."

"What a stickler you are."

"Why the hell not?"

"Uh . . . the honeymoon?"

"We've had that. We're calmer now. We can handle a marriage now and it'll be better on our first anniversary."

She lifted her eyebrows. "Not until then?"

With logic he expounded, "We'll leave the baby with my parents and go off by ourselves."

Soberly, she looked off across the water with eyes that were very serious.

"What's the matter with a delayed honeymoon?"

Turning back to him, again teary-eyed, she accused, "You want to abandon the baby."

"I never said that! I just said we'd have a vacation alone . . . like a honeymoon."

Very gently, she said with kindness, almost nostalgia, "You already know me better than any man has."

And quite honestly, he observed, "I don't see how that could be."

And she blew up. She was furious! She turned abruptly and stormed off, back down the beach and away from him.

He was astonished. He was turned back, his hands were on his hips and he was calling, "What the hell is the matter with you now!"

Wrong wording—altogether wrong.

Zach caught up with Jessica almost right away, and she told him through clenched teeth and in a fury, "Get away from me!"

She shocked him. He didn't know exactly how to handle her; she was two-thirds pregnant and really furious. He couldn't just sling her over his shoulder and take her home, pitch her on a bed and make love to her the way he wanted. Making love with a woman is a man's idea of bonding.

But there *are* men who take women in hate. They are cruel and mean and only take a dominant victory of release from women. There is no love.

And Zach wondered, was that how Jess had gotten pregnant? Some man just wanted sex and used her? Why would she wait for a commitment from such a man? Where was he? Zack would neuter him.

She was so furious, she wasn't speaking to him. But he managed to walk almost alongside her back to her house.

She told him to go away any number of times. There wasn't anything else she could do that wouldn't cause the town to gradually meld into a roaring donny-brook and throw Zach out of the county.

As much as she was furious with him at that time, she did not care to have him exiled from Sea View. Not yet.

At her door, Zach reached ahead of her and opened the screen door and stood aside as he pushed back the unlocked wooden front door. She went inside and tried to close the door, but he got his blocking foot in the door in time.

She said to Zach, "Leave me alone."

"I'll just be in the living room, reading yesterday's news."

With some stony, sober-faced patience, Zack took off his jacket and put it on the hall tree. From under his eyelashes, he slid his glance over to her. She was thin-lipped and furious. He went into the living room, found the paper and sat down.

The paper lay on his lap and he didn't read it. He thought what a calm person Hannah had been, and why couldn't Jessica be just close to that peace? She was a thunderhead.

Within his own head, he clearly heard Hannah's bubbling laughter. Even Mike's laugh came into his head.

Did they know what he was doing? If he concentrated enough, could they tell him who the bastard was who'd gotten Jessica pregnant?

He felt amusement fill his head.

Why would they be...amused...by Jessica being pregnant? He studied on that for some time.

He was still trying to figure why his dead wife and son would be amused by Jess's circumstances, when she came into the living room.

He rose, automatically courteous. And he watched her with cautious eyes.

At best, pregnant women are unpredictable. They can do anything, like burst into tears, or get hostile or go into a decline. Pregnant women are not stable people.

He didn't even say anything at all. He bit his tongue *not* to say, *Are you over your snit?* It probably wouldn't be the smart thing to say at that moment.

So he waited.

Stonily, she stood still, watching him in a studying way.

He figured she was deciding whether or not he was a moron. That was not in being a teacher way, or a human way but with women. There are echelons in everything. To Jessica, Zachary Thomas could be a male moron. It was an astonishing realization for a teacher.

So Zach wondered if Hannah had ever looked at him in the studying way that Jessica Channing was looking at him at that very moment. Jess was very maturely intent, and he wondered if she was discarding him.

He found that he earnestly did not want to be discarded.

What could he say to defend himself when he wasn't sure what the indictment was?

All he had said was that he didn't believe he knew Jessica Channing as well as a couple of other men.

That was an honest response. He hadn't known her for very long in actual time. But with his words, Jess had blown up and was really, really angry with him.

She stood there, probably deciding if she was going to reject him. Maybe she was deciding why she had allowed him to be around her at all. Or she could be balancing the odds on what kind of man he was.

He looked back at her soberly and with great intenseness. He would vocally reject any discarding she did on him. He wanted to be her only man. He wanted Jessica Channing for life and love and companionship.

She said, "Go home."

Very carefully, he told her, "I have the rest of the weekend."

"Use it to go back to Indiana."

"Jess, I love you."

"We'll see."

"When?"

By then, her enunciation had become familiar. She said, "Next spring."

"Don't close me out."

Very neutral, she replied levelly, "I haven't. I've invited you to come down next spring."

"Will you still let me call you?"

She watched him for almost too long before she replied, "Once a week."

"Twice." His quick response tromped on her last word.

Again, there was a long pause before Jess said, "We'll see."

"I'll fix supper." He started busily for the kitchen.

"No. I want you to leave now."

He stopped and looked at his pregnant love. "Let's go out to eat."

"No." And she enunciated it a second time, "I want you to leave now."

"How can you be so angry with me that you want me away from you?"

And she looked at him. Her eyes were yet again filled with tears. She replied, "We need space between us at this time. Go home."

"I don't need the space. I need you."

"Like every other man who's propositioned me?"

"I only meant that having shared sex with you, I had no other knowledge of you than the other men with whom you'd shared. I meant only that. You know I love you. I need to know if you will marry me. The baby will need a good daddy. I've had training. I believe I could be better with this baby than I was with Mike."

"Come back next spring."

Zach chose his words with additional care. "I feel a great need to be with you. I don't want to leave and not come back again for half a year. That's too long."

"Go away for now." Her tears brimmed.

"Let me come back tomorrow." His husky voice was tender. "I can't have you this upset without seeing to it that you are all right."

"No. It isn't wise. Go home."

"How can I do as you direct me, when I'm positive that you need me? How can you reject my love when you need a man to help you in this time?" He opened out his hands. "You need me. I want to be responsible for you. I want to be your husband and take care of you."

"That's too much of a burden for a stranger, at this time. I can take care of myself. It's too soon after Hannah's death for you to marry. As a teacher, it would be a scandal. It could hamper you or your future."

"I can do many things. Teaching is just one."

"You should be a good example for the kids."

"Kids are smarter now."

"They're mostly unruly. They need better discipline and more stringent rules to follow. The children, here, would be shocked if you married me now."

"How will knowing you're unwed and pregnant affect them?"

"It will. I . . . don't want you . . . involved."

He looked up and his eyes opened nakedly vulnerable. "You're protecting *me?*"

"This is important."

"It's madness! I'm an adult male, and I can take care of you."

She became more upset. Her words were of indignation. "It's too soon! Listen to what I say to you. It's too soon! Go home!"

"Ah, Jessie, let me hug you. I can't stand it. I need to hug you."

She gulped a sob, and he just went to her and took her rigid, lumpy body against his and held her. She bawled softly, conscious of neighbors. She hiccuped and her breaths shivered. She clung to him!

That gladdened his heart. He made soothing sounds and his hands held and smoothed back her hair. He was so darling that they went to bed together and he made careful love to her . . . again.

It was some time later, as they lay sprawled, lax and replete, that she asked him, "Why are you in my bed?"

He lay exhausted with his eyes closed and replied through weak lips, "I don't know."

"You did it to me again."

He opened one careful eye and asked with equal care, "What?"

"You're in my bed."

"No, not 'again,' because you've always had me in the guest room. This is the first time you let me bring you in here. The bed smells like you."

She tasted the word with some hostility, "Smell."

"Ummm." With great effort he managed to explain, "It has your fragrance."

"How do you mean that?"

He reached out an arm and drew her against his side. "Like you. It's heaven. I feel as if I'm on a cloud of pure delight."

She said, "Go home."

He put his one arm under her shoulders and the other across her rib cage and said, "I *am* home. Home is where the heart is, and mine's here with you."

"Go back to Indiana."

He lay silently except for several long, drawn-out sighs. Then he said, "You need a wider variety of retorts. You can say, *I like you in my bed with me. I like to breathe your male odor on my sheets. I love it that you love me!* Those are a few of the responses you can give me. After you learn them, we can expand your comments to me."

"Go back to Indiana."

"That's talking in a rut. Get out of the rut and say something different." He lifted his eyebrows and waited with great expectation.

"You've outstayed your welcome."

He hugged her. "I like your welcome. Wait until I recover enough and you can welcome me again."

"Go h—back to Indiana."

He sighed rather dramatically and put the back of his forearm across his forehead. "I am boggled by the realization that—"

"You do realize you ought to go on home."

"No. I just realize that you are so limited. It's a good thing I'm a teacher. We'll have to start out with communication and— It had just occurred to me that I don't remember if I paid any attention at all to whether or not you can cook. Do you?"

She retorted, "Brilliantly."

"Are you sure? I was so bemused by you that I can't actually say what sort of food I've had with you. Do you suppose I need to find out? What if I committed myself to training your conversational output and find that instead I ought to be giving you cooking lessons!"

"I'm a superb cook."

Cautiously, he inquired with great care, "What sort of cooking?"

"Peanut butter sandwiches."

He gasped rather too dramatically. "You do peanut butter sandwiches—all by yourself?"

"Yes."

"Well, I must say, that is a relief. I do hate the cooking time."

"Did you teach Hannah to cook?"

"It was not necessary, her mother did it before I was anywhere around." Then he added, "She also cleaned the house." And he had the gall to reach out a finger and swipe it along the bedside table.

She watched him as he examined the finger. With some satisfaction, he said, "It's clean. You're probably a good cook, too. If you do peanut butter sandwiches, I'll be okay." He settled down to lie on his side. He arranged her so that he was close and her head was on his shoulder. With a contented sigh, he told her, "It's nice to get a woman who has been programmed to respond and can cook and clean."

"Pah!"

He pulled back his head and asked in shock, "Who forgot about the sass part?"

"It would *not* be a good idea for you to marry so soon after you've lost Hannah. It could be for loneliness and just to fill your life. People in Indy who loved Hannah would be shocked and hostile."

"Maybe. But in coming to know you, they would change."

She said it with gentle firmness. "I'll see you next spring. Go back to Indiana."

In an earnest, low voice, he told her, "Jess, don't put me out of your life for six months. I can't stay away from you that long. I want to see you and watch you and hold you. Don't send me away like that. Let me be around you. If you don't want to get married until after the baby's here, I could probably handle that well enough, but I have to see you now and then."

He then went very serious and asked, "Would you come up and stay with me?"

"Good gravy, Zach, think what the people in that school would think of you! We can't do that! And it wouldn't be a good example for the kids."

"In these days, kids have seen just about everything. They adjust well."

"It could influence them."

He considered that seriously enough, but then he said, "Maybe."

She shook her head. "No question. Kids are influenced by what adults do. We need to behave better."

He turned and leaned over her to look into her eyes. "You are concerned how the kids here will feel if you marry while you're pregnant."

"Yes. You are known here. There'll be another meeting for you with Eileen who was given Mike's heart. The kids know you. It wouldn't be right for them to believe you'd do anything so rash as to make me pregnant."

"Who was the man?"

"Perhaps, someday, I'll tell you."

After a thoughtful pause, he promised her, "I won't kill him."

"I'm glad of that." She smiled and, being pregnant, her eyes teared.

"You're a very special woman. I want to take care of you."

"You might," she admitted. "Come back next spring, and we'll see."

So he again made tender love with her, being careful of her, almost too careful because Jessica's hunger was rampant.

When they again lay replete, he said, "Let me come for Christmas."

"Don't. You know it would be foolish. Do as I ask of you."

"We're close friends." He said that, lying naked in her bed. "Don't shut me out."

"We'll be talking to each other every week."

"Is that enough for you? It sounds very stingy and mean."

"Spring will come." She had her fingers in his hair and was making curls there.

He could feel the baby move against his stomach. "Do you mind being pregnant?"

"No."

"When we get married, will you let me give you another baby?"

She smiled just a little over his "another." He'd given her the first one, too. She said, "Yes."

"I'd like to see what one of my own would be like with you. I'll love this baby. No doubt about that. But I would like one by me."

"Yes."

"I love you, Jessica Channing."

With watery sentiment, she told him, "I believe I could love you very much."

And like the fat cat he was, he said with satisfaction, "See to it."

Ten

Zachary slowly got up from Jessica's bed and began to dress.

She watched him with the stupidly annoying tears filling her eyes.

He asked, "Why do you cry when you've told me to leave—how many times?"

"I'll miss you."

So he got back into her bed and held her close to him. It was very emotional. It was a different emotion. It was one of bonding.

When Zach finally said a gentle, reluctant goodbye to Jessica and departed from her house, he didn't immediately leave the town of Sea View. He drove his rented car over to Paul's house.

They talked for a short time, and the exchange was at first stilted and a bit hostile on Paul's part. But what Zach wanted was for Paul to call him the very minute Jess knew she was delivering. He made Paul swear on his honor. That was the stipulation.

Paul guessed, "She doesn't want you here."

"I think she's a little adamant with me on this...undertaking. She'll think the town will label *me* with being the bastard who got her pregnant. She is a little shy. I don't know who the bastard is, but if I ever find him, I'll rearrange his face."

"Oh?" With some snide questioning, Paul asked, "How will you manage to—arrange to do that?"

And Zach looked off as he replied, "I know, Paul. I may be a schoolteacher, but I can handle another man." Then he looked into Paul's eyes. "And I'll enjoy every blow."

With a glance at Zach, Paul asked, "Every blow—to you?"

"I probably wouldn't even feel those," Zach replied thoughtfully. "Not right away. I'd be so taken with hitting him. Do you know the guy?"

"More than likely."

Zach urged, "Tell me who you suspect."

"That's up to Jess."

In a deadly voice, Zach replied, "He's a bastard and after I get through with him, he'll be a bloody bastard."

Paul had no reply. But with the exchange, Paul's liking opened to Zach.

When Zach phoned Jess the next week, she asked, "Why were you talking to Paul?"

There is just nothing like the gossip in a little town. Zach replied honestly, "I wanted to know who was the man and if he'd ever come to see you."

She was silent for a time before she carefully asked, "And...what did Paul say?"

"He just nodded." Then Zach added, "The guy does know you're in this fix."

"Yes."

"Paul's a gossip."

She demurred. "He cares about the people in Sea View and—"

"He ought to pay more attention to his wife—"

She protested, "They already have three kids—"

But he finished his sentence, "—and help her out now and then!"

"Yes, I could see him doing that."

Zach admitted honestly, "I should have helped more with Mike."

"He was one child and could have used a father's guiding, but Paul's got three kids."

"You act like three is a mob of kids."

"Your time will come."

In surprise, he exclaimed, "How many kids are we going to have?"

"We'll see."

And he was mush.

But he remembered later she'd been told that—before he had left Sea View—he had spoken to Paul. In a small town, nothing was private. And only that made him wonder how many people in Sea View realized he and Jessica were lovers.

And then Zach thought perhaps Jess had been right to delay their marriage. But such a decision gave him a pang of remorse.

He sat and thought about it. He was lost in seeing the empty time coming up between them for the sake of *his* reputation. She would go through this ordeal alone in order for him to seem untouched. What about her? What about Jessica Channing, unwed mother? She was something special.

So...how "special" was he? And he pondered that. His lengthy self-examination brought Zach to the conclusion that he wasn't at all special, and Jessica shouldn't be alone when the kid arrived.

He'd go back to Sea View then.

And while he was there, he'd just look around and see if he could find the bastard who was responsible for giving Jess that baby. One good clip on his jaw and another telling punch to his beer belly maybe would be enough to sooth Zach's indignation.

Or was it maybe his possessiveness?

Ahhh. Was it indignation for Jess's situation or was it just his own control and possessiveness? That was interesting to consider. Was he really that indignant that some other man had gotten Jess pregnant—or was he just jealous the baby wasn't his own?

He remembered how hot she'd been when he'd come back. She was already pregnant. Pregnant women often were voraciously, sexually hungry. They were already caught and therefore had no hesitation? Their bodies were hungry? Women were strange.

And his attention went to dwell on the difference between the stable men and the unstable women. Why were women so baffling and unpredictable? Who knew? They never followed directions or rules. But they always drove the same way and never varied their routes. Life would be easier if women were more like men . . . mentally.

Instead of saying, "No," they'd say, "Now."

Life would be a whole lot easier.

It rapidly became apparent that Jess was too far away from Zach. He missed her. He was quiet and kind and a little vague. His students worried about him. Too many asked, "Are you okay?"

The principal snagged Zach to quiz him. He began with his usual tact. He asked, "Well, you might as well admit what the hell is happening with you that you're so moony. It's got to be a woman."

And before Zach remembered his careful conduct, he replied, "Yeah."

"Who and where?"

"TEXAS. Did you know you are supposed to always say and write that in capital letters?"

"Yes. Those pushy TEXANS never let up." The principal watched Zach. He knew, of course, that Zach had lost his family in some little hick town in Tex—TEXAS. Just last spring.

Although the principal waited for Zach's reply, Zach didn't say anything else.

But the principal was a good, honest man who didn't gossip. He never said a word to anyone else.

So when Paul called Zach at eleven o'clock on December third, and at four after eleven when Zach called the principal and said he had to go to TEXAS, the principal just said, "Okay."

"It could be a while. A week or so."

"You got the time?"

Zach admitted, "Maybe not."

"We'll figure something out."

"Thanks."

As would happen, it did take only several hours for Zach to get to Sea View. He'd been so lucky on schedules all the way that he never exclaimed even inside his brain that it was all working his way.

Sometimes things don't work at all.

But within just under three hours, Zach was landing on the little airfield outside Sea View in one of Houston's shuttle planes.

And Paul was there to take Zach to the hospital.

Zach got into Paul's car asking, "She delivered yet?"

"Not the last I heard—" he looked at his watch "—five minutes ago."

"Hurry."

"Zach," Paul said very, very patiently, "we're almost already there. One of the volunteers is already watching for you."

"How'd you do that?"

With great, sleepy care the father of three told Zach, "It's a little town."

They said no more until Paul turned a hyper Zach over to a charming, smiling aid. Paul left with a soft "Good luck."

They were words that Zach didn't even hear, because he was so riveted on getting to Jess.

Paul's good wishes were needed. There had been odd delaying complications that caused some intense attention, great puzzlement and the gathering of several other doctors, one coming in by plane from Corpus.

With Zach's arrival, everything seemed to smooth out, and he was even allowed into the delivery room after he was scrubbed and gowned and masked.

Her parents, kin and friends all allowed that without any argument.

It was Zach who got to hold the baby! They gave that little, redheaded girl-miracle to Zach! And he was surprised that he still knew how to hold one that little. She was perfect. She looked like a baby angel.

Tears leaked out of Zach's eyes as he told an out-cold Jessica, "She's almost as beautiful as you! Look at her! My God! Oh, Jessica, you made a beauty here. We'll have trouble with little boys and adolescents and grown males all of our lives!"

So saying, he'd already told the whole, entire hospital—which spilled it over the whole town—that Zachary Thomas was going to be around Sea View, but more specifically, around Jessica Channing for some time to come.

There he was, in the middle of the night, acting like Jess's baby was...his.

And there were those who questioned: Was he serious or just using Jess? Was _he_ the father? He must be. And there were women who retorted, "He could just love her that much and is man enough to stand by her."

Zach never did sleep. He sat by Jessica and held her hand. When he had to relieve himself, her mother or daddy spelled him. But the unconscious Jessica knew the difference and she fretted until he returned.

Zach smiled kindly at Cynthia Channing as he gently told Jess's own mother, "She depends on me."

Cynthia Channing only looked at Zach. She knew who he was.

It was late morning before Jess stirred and really, actually wakened. She looked at Zach, sitting beside her, holding her hand. He was groggy, a little rumpled. And he needed a shower and shave. He was gorgeous. He looked like a second-class highwayman.

Jessica asked, "Zach? Zach?"

"I'm here, love. You have a perfect little girl. She's redheaded. I couldn't see her eyes."

And Jess exclaimed, "I *dreamed* you were here! I dreamed you were here!"

"I was talking you through it," Zach told her with the élan of a glider pilot. He'd that easily pushed aside the need of all the experts, who'd worked their tails off, and Zach stood alone in Jess's consciousness. He was there. He was all that mattered.

So Zach stayed for two weeks. On the phone, he told the principal back in Indiana, "I'm needed here."

How can anyone ignore such a statement? Actually, Zach wasn't needed anywhere but at his classes! He was out-and-out *useless* at Jess's house.

He held the baby. He fed her if she just opened her little rosebud lips. He changed her with some show-offiness. He claimed he knew all about babies. Fortunately, Grandmother Cynthia was there.

So were Jess's sister, sister-in-law, her bridge bunch, the hotel's female staff, cousins and even out-of-towner relatives and more friends. There were more than enough friends. It was a toss-up whether the out-of-towners were there to see Jess or the baby...or just to watch that Zachary Thomas person.

The visitors looked at Zach soberly and some even squinted their eyes a little. The men rubbed their noses while they spoke a sentence or two to each other as they shifted their feet and stood off, aside from the women. They were watching and discussing Zach.

The women scurried around. The men visited among themselves.

One man had the gall to intrusively suggest in an aside to Zach, warning him, "Begin as you plan to go on."

Zach shifted the baby to his other arm and asked, "You from Sea View or from on out beyond?" He was getting some TEXAS shine.

Jess's sister and sister-in-law eyed each other in communication. And Jess's sister whispered, "I just hope he marries her."

"Why?"

Slowly serious, someone close by replied, "Not married, this way, as she is now, she'd be a target for any hungry man."

Zach came through the door at just that time and he stopped, staring at the women. Then he turned back to look at Jessica, sitting in the rocker by her bed and holding her baby, watching the little miracle.

Zach looked at the suddenly silent women and asked, "Did the man ever come near here in all this time? Does he know about the baby?"

They all shook their heads. All the women. The silent, still men just watched Zach.

Zach nodded and told the listening, riveted gathering, "He didn't ever come around here to see her. He hasn't even inquired about her." Zach had dismissed the man as useless.

It was several days when he judged that Jessica was strong enough to hear it when Zach told her, "He didn't come here to see if you were all right. Nor did he ever look at the Princess."

How did Jess reply to that? She smiled at her lover and told him, "You were here. You probably terrified any other man who might think I'm easy."

He could agree to that.

It tore Zach in two to leave Jess. He had to go back to Indiana for the rest of the year. He was only over vacation time about two personal days. He could handle that.

He asked Paul, "Any good teaching jobs open around here?"

And Paul gave Zach a weighing evaluation before he probed, "You thinking about moving in?"

With a confidence that was a little eye-rolling, Zach shared, "We're thinking about getting married this spring. She wouldn't give me the honor until after the baby was here. Little Lucille Channing belongs to me."

"We all know that."

Zach nodded. "The bastard never once showed up."

Paul was dumbstruck and therefore silent.

So that segment of the conversation made the area male rounds with some hilarious astonishment. The local females weren't told; women were such gossips that they couldn't keep a secret.

* * *

So Zach went home. He called daily... to check in.

Zach coaxed that Jess come to Indiana and bring along the Princess. She demurred. They talked on the phone and made plans.

It was the end of January going into February that Jess reluctantly left the Princess in Sea View with her mother...her father, her other kin, her bridge club, her cousins and various friends. And Jess went solo up to Indiana to see Zach.

He had spent two weeks cleaning his house. He cleaned the oven, the motor on the washing machine, the lights outside by the backyard and the garage. It was snowing. His neighbors thought his lines had fallen under the weight of the snow.

He remembered to change the sheets.

On spring break, in Sea View, theirs was the wedding of the most garnered interest anyone could remember. And it was at that time when Zach's parents came to help witness the great event.

The senior Thomases were rock hunters out west. They dug into the primal hills and looked for specific kinds of rocks. They'd found little human bones trapped long, millions of years ago by sedimentation and big human bones that volcanoes had locked into eternity. It was fascinating.

Zach's parents looked very like the people who lived in tents as photographers. But they actually did rocks.

The senior Thomases made the townspeople look at Zach with puzzlement. He'd seemed rather to stand out like a sore thumb and his assimilation of facts had seemed flawed. But having met his parents, Zach began to look more like home folk.

The ceremony was quiet—actually, while it was intended to be closed and discreet, it was pretty raucous. The men, standing in groups aside, were especially hilarious. And there were jokes going the male rounds about the wedding night. The men's eyes would catch and the laughter would bubble.

Men are needed on this earth.

That is a sobering fact.

But they are a trial and an aggravation. For one thing, they don't really understand women. They are constantly amazed and stymied by them. They are lacking in the most basic understanding.

They never use the same road to go back somewhere, they always take a different way back and they invariably get lost, but they never ask for directions! Not unless there's a woman in the car they can send in somewhere to find out where the hell they are.

Men never realize what a trial they are to women. Each man thinks he's a prize. For women, there's no other choice. And that is one of the most stunning of all realizations.

On that day, Jessica married the father of her baby. He still didn't even suspect that. How could he not? Every other person there knew, why not the daddy?

The couple was married and tears leaked from Zach's eyes and he was one big, tender smile. He was mush. Jess wasn't much better.

With the ceremony, Zach insisted that the Princess be present to witness the fact that he was marrying her mother and therefore would be her father. Dumb. Just about everyone there knew what Zach didn't...yet know.

For the ceremony, Jessica wore a bridal gown that wasn't white. It was a very pale pink. She was gorgeous. Ethereal. She made all their smiles vulnerable. People like her were the reason other people married. She made it seem special.

And Zach contributed to that. He looked like the dream man women think men are. Or can be, with a little help and guidance. All women know how men ought to be...generally with considerable hopeful help, which is so carelessly rejected all along the way.

So Zach's mother, the senior Mrs. Thomas, sat during that ancient pagan rite of matrimony. Words. Admonitions, which only a few women heard. So Mrs. Thomas, Sr., examined the child on her lap who had been borne by her son's selected woman who would become their daughter-in-law.

That was when she made the discovery.

At the reception, at The Horizon Hotel, Zach's mother said to her son, "Why didn't you marry her at the time? In these days, it isn't kind to leave the woman alone."

And her precious son said, "Huh?"

Being a researcher and a woman of few words, his mother said, "The child is yours."

And again the teacher said, "Huh?"

With some gathered patience, his mother was more specific. "Her ear."

Cautiously, the son asked the mother who cracked rocks for bones, "Whose ear?"

"The Princess is your genetic offspring."

Saying that in a carrying voice, the mother was heard by most of the silenced gathering.

And Jessica Channing Thomas heard. She bit her smile and was silent.

In some astonishment, Zachary questioned, "I'm the father of the Princess?"

Placidly, Mrs. Thomas replied, "She has your ear. It goes from father to daughter to son. You have my father's ear. Mike was male and didn't get the gene. The Princess is female and got the gene. She's yours."

In stoned astonishment, her son Zachary asked his mother bluntly, "How can you tell?"

By then, the whole room's attention was on Mrs. Thomas and her son. So he whispered, "My ear?"

"Yes. See mine?" She put back her raven hair and showed the small separation of bone on the down-sliding inner fold. "It splits briefly. See the Princess's ear? Same ear, same split."

"It *is!*"

And he looked over to Jessica in stunned delight. "She's mine!"

Jess just stood there in her wedding gown with puddled eyes and a little smile.

Zach said, "Why didn't you tell me?"

And before that whole bunch of people, whose heads turned as in a tennis match, Jess said, "It was too soon after... the wreck."

And he gasped, "You're a... stickler!"

She shrugged in a very interesting way.

So Zach turned to Paul and said in astonishment, "*I'm* the bastard!"

And Paul laughed. "So hit yourself."

* * *

It was a very hilarious, strange and interesting wedding party. It really wasn't the solemn, studied traditional one. Exclamations were on the female side. The men already knew. But there were women who said, "I knew." They hadn't, actually, because they prefer to go with tradition, but there are those who try to seem knowledgeable about people.

No one believes them, but, being kind, they pretend to believe and they will even gasp, "You knew?" Having to deal with men, women are basically kind.

The party was a good one. For being rock breakers, his family fitted in quite well. It was a little unnerving that the paleontologists would hold arms and finger elbows. But their fingers never did search out vertebrae.

After some of the punch, Paul told Zach all the times he'd wanted to chide Zach into admitting he was the daddy of Jess's baby.

Zach asked, "How did you know?"

"Everybody in town knew. Jess went up to your room with you."

"You knew that? I never thought about that being what caught her. It was so quick that I didn't think of it as being potent. It wasn't even making love."

"It was adequate."

Zach replied, "Well, yes, I guess it certainly was! The Princess is mine!"

"What if it hadn't been the ear?" Paul asked. "What if there'd never been any clue that she was yours?"

"I'd have figured it out." Zach gestured. "She'd be a girl and she has mother's hair."

"Jess's redheaded."

"I had noticed."

"And her grandmother's ear."

Zach commented, "I suppose people can claim offspring in all kinds of ways. Manners and habits go along."

"Are you taking them to Indiana?" That wasn't Paul's voice, so Zach looked over at his brother-in-law Matthew and smiled. "No. I'm coming here. I believe there's an opening for a history teacher in the consolidated high school."

Matthew told Zach, "You can use my name when you apply."

Paul said, "And mine."

His own father offered, "We can give a seminar on rocks and bones."

Someone laughed, saying, "And Ears!"

The party lasted late. The Princess showed her ability in being a party girl by laughing and being sassy. It was then that Zach told Jess, who was clamped to his side, "She'll be a handful. We'll have to have a competitor right way."

But Jess said, "Not this year."

"Well, it was just so easy that I thought you'd jump at the chance!"

She looked at the ceiling.

And Zach told her earnestly, "You did a terrific job of her. She's really something."

Jess was generous. She reminded her new husband, "You gave her the one ear."

And he said, "Yeah." His smile was smug.

It wasn't until that summer when Zach had moved them all back to Sea View that the little harvester recipient, Eileen, came to Sea View for a checkup. It was she who carried Mike's heart inside her chest.

She was very different than her video at the gathering of recipients of the Harvest.

Jessica was with Zach as he met with Eileen at the hospital. Zach thought he was healed enough to handle meeting the girl and seeing her.

She was still skinny and growing like a weed. She was nine. She was bright and sassy and alive!

She told Zach, "Mike's inside me. He is so funny. He is so strong. Feel him."

She took Zach's hand and put it on her bony flat chest, and under his hand, Zach felt Mike's heart.

It was an emotional time of great awe. And it was Mike who lived on, too. Because of the harvest, Mike went on inside this vivacious little girl. Mike would be so amused to be part of a female.

Distracted by Mike's humor, it was a while until Zach could hear again. Eileen was saying, "And I jumped across. It was like flying. Mike is a good heart. Thank you."

They became friends. Eileen would come back for a checkup now and again, and she thought the Princess was a miracle.

So was she. So was Eileen.

And in that time, Jessica once said to Hannah's memory, "Ah, Hannah, do you understand him? Us? Can you tolerate our love?"

And a strange peace washed over Jessica.

* * *

All those people, in Sea View, lived in a muddle of gossip and hilarity with enough contention to spice things up. Zach and Jessica had three more kids, which were more than their quota for this fragile earth. They were all healthy and they loved each other—most of the time.

* * * * *

COMING NEXT MONTH

It's Silhouette Desire's 1000th birthday! Join us for a spectacular three-month celebration, starring your favorite authors and the hottest heroes of the decade!

#997 BABY DREAMS—Raye Morgan
The Baby Shower
Sheriff Rafe Lonewolf couldn't believe his feisty new prisoner was the innocent woman she claimed to be. But a passionate night with Cami Bishop was suddenly making *him* feel criminal!

#998 THE UNWILLING BRIDE—Jennifer Greene
The Stanford Sisters
Paige Stanford's new neighbor was sexy, smart...and single! Little did she know Stefan Michaelovich wanted to make *her* his blushing bride!

#999 APACHE DREAM BRIDE—Joan Elliott Pickart
When Kathy Maxwell purchased a dream catcher, she had no idea she'd soon catch herself an Apache groom! But could her dream really come true...or would she have to give up the only man she ever loved?

#1000 MAN OF ICE—Diana Palmer
Silhouette Desire #1000!
After one tempestuous night with irresistible Barrie Bell, May's MAN OF THE MONTH, Dawson Rutherford, swore off love forever. Now the only way he could get the land he wanted was to make Barrie his temporary bride.

#1001 INSTANT HUSBAND—Judith McWilliams
The Wedding Night
Nick St. Hilarion needed a mother for his daughter, not a woman for himself to love! But when Ann Lennon arrived special delivery, he realized he might not be able to resist falling for his mail-order wife!

#1002 BABY BONUS—Amanda Kramer
Debut Author
Leigh Townsend was secretly crazy about sexy Nick Romano, but she wasn't going to push him to propose! So she didn't tell him he was going to be a daddy—or else he would insist on becoming a husband, too.

MILLION DOLLAR SWEEPSTAKES
AND EXTRA BONUS PRIZE DRAWING

SILHOUETTE® Desire® CELEBRATION 1000

A treasured piece of romance could be yours!

During April, May and June as part of Desire's Celebration 1000 you can enter to win an original piece of art used on an actual Desire cover!

Or you could win one of 300 autographed Man of the Month books!

See Official Sweepstakes Rules for more details.

SILHOUETTE DESIRE® "CELEBRATION 1000" SWEEPSTAKES
OFFICIAL RULES—NO PURCHASE NECESSARY

To enter, complete an Official Entry Form or a 3"x5" card by hand printing "Silhouette Desire Celebration 1000 Sweepstakes," your name and address, and mail it to: In the U.S.: Silhouette Desire Celebration 1000 Sweepstakes, P.O. Box 9069, Buffalo, NY 14269-9069, or in Canada: Silhouette Desire Celebration 1000 Sweepstakes, P.O. Box 637, Fort Erie, Ontario L2A 5X3. Limit one entry per envelope. Entries must be sent via first-class mail and be received no later than 6/30/96. No liability is assumed for lost, late or misdirected mail.

Prizes: Grand Prize—an original painting (approximate value $1500 U.S.);300 Runner-up Prizes—an autographed Silhouette Desire® Book (approximate value $3.50 U.S./$3.99 CAN. each). Winners will be selected in a random drawing (to be conducted no later than 9/30/96) from among all eligible entries received by D.L. Blair, Inc., an independent judging organization whose decision is final.

Sweepstakes offer is open only to residents of the U.S. (except Puerto Rico) and Canada who are 18 years of age or older, except employees and immediate family members of Harlequin Enterprises Ltd., their affiliates, subsidiaries, and all agencies, entities and persons connected with the use, marketing or conduct of this sweepstakes. All federal, state, provincial, municipal and local laws apply. Offer void where prohibited by law. Taxes and/or duties are the sole responsibility of the winners. Any litigation within the province of Quebec respecting the conduct and awarding of prizes may be submitted to the Regie des alcools des courses et des jeux. All prizes will be awarded; winners will be notified by mail. No substitution for prizes is permitted. Odds of winning are dependent upon the number of eligible entries received.

Grand Prize winner must sign and return an Affidavit of Eligibility within 30 days of notification. In the event of noncompliance within this time period, prize may be awarded to an alternate winner. Any prize or prize notification returned as undeliverable may result in the awarding of that prize to an alternate winner. By acceptance of their prize, winners consent to the use of their names, photographs or likenesses for purposes of advertising, trade and promotion on behalf of Harlequin Enterprises Ltd., without further compensation unless prohibited by law. In order to win a prize, residents of Canada will be required to correctly answer a time-limited arithmetical skill-testing question administered by mail.

For a list of winners (available after October 31, 1996) send a separate self-addressed stamped envelope to: Silhouette Desire Celebration 1000 Sweepstakes Winners, P.O. Box 4200, Blair, NE 68009-4200.

SWEEPR

BEGINNING IN April
FROM

▼ SILHOUETTE®

Desire®

DEBUT AUTHOR

In April, May and June we'll be celebrating the publication of Silhouette Desire's 1000th book! And each month will feature a brand-new writer you're sure to be excited about.

In April—
TWO WEDDINGS AND A BRIDE by Anne Eames

In May—
BABY BONUS by Amanda Kramer

In June—
THE LONER AND THE LADY by Eileen Wilks

Don't miss these stars of tomorrow— premiering today!

Plus, each Debut Author book has a bonus! Double Pages & Privileges Proofs of Purchase! Get more rewards—faster!

As seen on TV!
Free Gift Offer

With a Free Gift proof-of-purchase from any Silhouette® book, you can receive a beautiful cubic zirconia pendant.

This gorgeous marquise-shaped stone is a genuine cubic zirconia—accented by an 18" gold tone necklace.

(Approximate retail value $19.95)

Send for yours today...
compliments of ▼ *Silhouette*®

To receive your free gift, a cubic zirconia pendant, send us one original proof-of-purchase, photocopies not accepted, from the back of any Silhouette Romance™, Silhouette Desire®, Silhouette Special Edition®, Silhouette Intimate Moments® or Silhouette Shadows™ title available in February, March or April at your favorite retail outlet, together with the Free Gift Certificate, plus a check or money order for $1.75 U.S./$2.25 can. (do not send cash) to cover postage and handling, payable to Silhouette Free Gift Offer. We will send you the specified gift. Allow 6 to 8 weeks for delivery. Offer good until April 30, 1996 or while quantities last. Offer valid in the U.S. and Canada only.

Free Gift Certificate

Name: _____

Address: _____

City: _____ State/Province: _____ Zip/Postal Code: _____

Mail this certificate, one proof-of-purchase and a check or money order for postage and handling to: SILHOUETTE FREE GIFT OFFER 1996. In the U.S.: 3010 Walden Avenue, P.O. Box 9057, Buffalo NY 14269-9057. In Canada: P.O. Box 622, Fort Erie,

---

FREE GIFT OFFER
ONE PROOF-OF-PURCHASE

079-KBZ-R

To collect your fabulous FREE GIFT, a cubic zirconia pendant, you must include this original proof-of-purchase for each gift with the properly completed Free Gift Certificate.

079-KBZ-R

Also available by popular author

LASS SMALL

Silhouette Desire®

#05755	BEWARE OF WIDOWS	$2.89	☐
#05817	*TWEED	$2.99	☐
#05830	A NEW YEAR	$2.99	☐
#05848	I'M GONNA GET YOU	$2.99	☐
#05860	SALTY AND FELICIA	$2.99 U.S.	☐
		$3.50 CAN.	☐
#05895	AN OBSOLETE MAN	$2.99 U.S.	☐
		$3.50 CAN.	☐

*Man of the Month

Yours Truly™

#52004	NOT LOOKING FOR A TEXAS MAN	$3.50 U.S.	☐
		$0.99 CAN.	☐

(limited quantities available on certain titles)

TOTAL AMOUNT	$
POSTAGE & HANDLING	$
($1.00 for one book, 50¢ for each additional)	
APPLICABLE TAXES**	$_____
TOTAL PAYABLE	$_____
(check or money order—please do not send cash)	

To order, complete this form and send it, along with a check or money order for the total above, payable to Silhouette Books, to: **In the U.S.:** 3010 Walden Avenue, P.O. Box 9077, Buffalo, NY 14269-9077; **In Canada:** P.O. Box 636, Fort Erie, Ontario, L2A 5X3.

Name: _____

Address: _____ City: _____

State/Prov.: _____ Zip/Postal Code: _____

**New York residents remit applicable sales taxes.
  Canadian residents remit applicable GST and provincial taxes.   SLSBACK7

Silhouette®

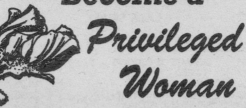

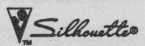